Also by Jennifer Gresko

Jane Has Cancer

Lullabies, Liquor and Late Nights

Love After Fifth Avenue

Jennifer Gresko

Gresko Publishing House
2013

First Printing: 2013

ISBN: 978-1-329-00067-4

*For my two beautiful girls who let me
daydream from time to time and make the world
an entertaining place to live.
You are the true meaning of love and joy.*

Chapter 1…

I stood there trembling, a hundred eyes burning a hole into the back of my skull. My knees were beginning to buckle underneath the weight of the question still fluttering around my head. My focus was on the yellow candle dripping hot wax all over the crisp white tablecloth.

In my dreams, I had envisioned this moment about a thousand times; the fancy restaurant, the crowd of people, the velvety black box with the most beautiful diamond ring shining out of it.

Yes, this was the moment I had been waiting for since I was a little girl; twirling around my bedroom, draped in a white sheet with my strawberry shortcake pillowcase "veil" bouncing on my head. Only, in my dreams, when the white knight climbed off of his steed, knelt down on one knee before me and mouthed the four most anticipated words in the history of romance, I said YES!

And now, standing here, with the entire room gawking at me, looking into the eyes of this beautiful man with his knee pushed down into the plush carpet of the nicest Italian restaurant in the city, holding his heart and a diamond ring in his hand, I couldn't muster up anything more than a whispered, "Oh!"

His hand was shaking, clinging to the edge of the table to keep his balance, and I knew that he wouldn't move until I said something. Out loud at least.

This was the plan right, the next mark on my life's checklist? Find my Prince Charming and allow him to sweep me off of my proverbial feet. We would have loads of adorable babies and live happily ever after in his shiny, fairy tale castle. Well, more like his penthouse apartment in Manhattan, but a castle, by most standards, nonetheless.

It had been my dream for the past twenty four years. So why, when I was this close to sealing the deal on my every fantasy, was my body betraying me, leaving me speechless and paralyzed.

"Did she say yes?" an older blonde woman sitting in a booth next to us whispered. The man with her just shook his head and I could again feel all of the eyes around me. Everyone was eager to know what was happening, as if they were our closest friends.

Finally, I met Charlie's gaze and could see the frightened look on his handsome face. My stunned silence had apparently not gone unnoticed.

Charlie was the epitome of masculinity. His golden sandy colored hair, his bronze chiseled physique; he looked as if he was ripped off the front of one of those dirty romance novel covers, wind-blown and holding a damsel in distress.

And, oh, those smoldering dark eyes!

Eyes that were at this very moment, as vulnerable as a newborn baby in the path of a speeding train (me being the train). Those eyes, fixed on me and desperately waiting for me to tell him that I would be spending the rest of my life with him. And I couldn't get my mouth to speak.

I met Charlie almost two years ago, walking through Central Park at precisely 7:15pm. I remember the time so vividly because I was exactly fifteen minutes late catching my tour bus back home to the quiet streets of Lancaster County, PA.

I was on a day trip to the Big Apple, seeing all of the "Sights, Lights and Frights that NYC had to offer," or so the brochure had read. I knew it was a bad idea to come alone, *and* to wander off without the group, but I always seemed to do foolish things like that. I probably should have been tragically killed or mauled by a bear or something already, but it was the crazy parts that made life all the more exciting, right?

I had spent hours wandering aimlessly around Central Park, immersed in the magic it emanated. Venetian gondola rides at the Boathouse, ice skating and carousel rides hidden away from the hustle and bustle of the city, and the utterly enchanting horse drawn carriages clip-clopping along the paths. It was every hopeless romantic girl's dream world. Naturally, I was in heaven.

That was, up until I rounded a corner and found myself on a dark pathway that I was quite certain was not leading me back to where the crowded bus filled with wide-eyed tourists had dropped me off this morning.

I darted around the shadowy twists and turns of the pathway, looking for the tour group, the bus, or any signs of civilization whatsoever. My feet couldn't keep up with my body and my strappy sandal, which I had already discovered was a terrible idea for a "walking tour," came loose and a pebble smaller than a dime changed my situation forever.

Destroying every ounce of balance I had been struggling to keep and tossing it into the darkness, my ankle twisted to the right, forcing my knees to buckle.

Bracing myself for the pain of smashing into the pavement, I closed my eyes as my arms caught hold of something warm and soft and I found myself wrapped in the embrace of an incredibly sweet smelling stranger.

As I lifted my face up, my eyes locked with the most beautiful crescent shaped brown eyes I had ever seen. From that first look, I felt as if he could see right through to my soul.

Without letting go of my unsteady arms, he firmly planted me back onto the ground and said, "Sorry, I didn't mean to embarrass you," clearly noticing my flushed cheeks. "I just couldn't bear to see that beautiful face get damaged by these filthy park streets."

That was how our story began.

Hopelessly romantic.

I literally fell for him.

It was all a big fairy tale, like every love story you'd find in the movies. Small town girl meets handsome wealthy businessman and they fall madly in love.

Perfection, right?

Then, why was I here, at this restaurant, staring into those eyes I had more than once gotten completely lost in, unable to speak?

Having to say something to kill the silence, I forced out, "Please Charlie, let's talk."

Those crescent eyes immediately shattered and closed as the hand holding the shimmering diamond ring fell to his side. That wasn't the answer he was looking for. He dropped his other knee to the ground so that he was no longer kneeling; just a crumpled pile of designer clothes on the floor.

I could hear all of the gasps and whispers from the disappointed intruders of what should have been a very private moment. Some of them might even have recognized Charlie, being a wealthy eligible bachelor and head honcho at one of the most prestigious law firms in New York.

And who was I? I was the girl saying no when every other girl in here would've said yes in the blink of an eye. Even I would've kicked myself if I was in their shoes.

"Please, sit here with me," I gently pleaded with him as the tears finally started to roll down my cheeks.

He didn't lift his head, just slowly rose off his knees and slid into his seat, completely broken and humiliated. He was not the kind of man who experienced disappointment often. I never wanted him to feel that way either. I loved him so much. So much I would have done anything for him, anything but this.

I slid down in my own chair across the table from this man that I had just destroyed with one wrong answer. I could still feel the stares from everyone in the restaurant. The waiters waiting to storm our table with a bottle of celebratory champagne had fallen back, like soldiers in a losing war, not daring to interrupt this conversation we were about to have.

Charlie stared at the now closed velvet box he was twirling in his hands, as if all of his hopes and dreams were enclosed in that little box I had just rejected. I guess, in a way, they were.

I had no idea what to say. What could make all of this better? Instead of words, I sobbed into the napkin that was in my lap, wishing more than anything we wouldn't have an audience for this awkwardness.

In the beginning of our relationship, everything felt perfect. Knight in shining armor and all that, right? So, it was easy to pick a weed or two from our garden of love, like him missing dinner because of a late meeting or me not wanting to go to another boring cocktail party for one of his business partners.

Those were small problems that one hellacious kiss could melt away and be forgotten. That was all he had to do, just put those delicious lips on mine and I was butter. Those kisses carried us through many rough nights. You couldn't deny that we had fireworks.

Nevertheless, you get to the end of those fireworks at some point and are immersed in the smoky mess left behind in its wake. And when the smoke finally clears and the brilliant lights are no longer visible in the sky, you have nothing but the empty dark night.

Charlie worked entirely too much, way more than I had ever imagined. It was different when I had a life and a job, but I had left all of that to be with him. I was becoming less enchanted by the big city and spending more time alone than with the man I moved here to be with.

My best friend Amy would call me every week, begging me to tell her all of the fabulous stories of my new exciting life. She was a small town girl, born and raised like me, and was almost as breathless as I was about my whirlwind romance. She loved her life, but thought of it as a tuna sandwich when compared to the filet mignon she believed my life to be. It was a true Cinderella story in her eyes. We were such suckers for the classics.

I just wasn't able to burst her fantasy bubble by telling her how life had changed for us after I moved here. I always glamorized everything we did so that she could have her vicarious daydreams. I guess I had spent too many years with my nose planted in romance novels to realize that riding off into the sunset wasn't a real life ending.

The books always stopped right before they told you how the handsome man leaves his dirty socks on the bathroom floor and no one in town wants to buy jewelry from anyone without the word "Tiffany" on the box. The small town Cinderella is left to do the chores again and her hopes and dreams go out the door.

I thought maybe we were just going through a rough patch. Everybody goes through rough patches. It couldn't be perfect all the time. Even though they never talked about it in the story books, I'm sure Cinderella made a few dinners that got cold waiting for the prince while he was off doing royal things. I mean, he had a kingdom to run, he couldn't be stuck in the castle with Cinderella all day, romancing her while the country was left to fend for itself.

But those couple of bad weeks turned into a couple bad months, and Charlie and I grew further and further from those hopeful people that were so much in love.

All of the reasons and the past few months of feeling like I had made the wrong decision, moving away from everything I had ever known, had led both of us to this restaurant, forced into a choice that would either make or break us forever. Obviously, my non-answer foretold the way it was going to go.

I looked once more at Charlie's face, his hand still held out in front of him, begging me not to say everything we both already knew. I had assumed that he was stopping me from giving him an excuse, but I now realized he was stopping me from admitting the truth.

His eyes had changed from shocked to a more empathetic acknowledgement. I could only guess that he was re-enacting all of our moments in his head, just as I was. At first, I thought this whole evening came as an unexpected shock, but a small part of me realized that maybe this was coming for a long time.

Charlie was a very by the book kind of guy. Having been together nearly two years, enduring the good, the bad, and the very ugly, marriage was our natural course of action, our next step. He was the only partner in his firm who was still a bachelor and they were always pressing the "M" word into our conversations at parties and social events. As far as they knew, our lives were as perfect as one of God's rainbows. So what was the hold up?

People are always trying to fit you into the mold of their lives, maybe so they aren't the only ones. Our story just wasn't complete to them until I walked into an event with a huge sparkly ring on my finger and shared the news with the whole company. Then I could join in their matrimonial business world, like some Wall Street step-ford wife.

I could see it now. This "setback" for Charlie would be quietly brushed under the rug like a rogue dust bunny. The blonde, perfectly airbrushed women of the corporate circle couldn't help gossiping about how I was never quite good enough for a man like Charlie Cooper.

"Charlie, listen…" I managed to get past his unfaltering hand. He slowly put his palm on the table, never looking up at my face. "You know that I love you." For the first time in a long time, those words had a lot more meaning behind them. They also had power, and I watched as they stabbed Charlie in the chest. I couldn't stop now.

"We both know that things have been…wrong…the past few months, and I just think that…" Even though I knew it was the right thing to do, I couldn't pull the words out of my mouth.

Those words were final.

They meant that the fantasy was over. Our happy ending was gone.

No, I couldn't be the final word.

Before I had a chance to stumble over my own lips, Charlie spoke. His first words since that life-altering question.

"It's not working anymore." It wasn't a question. It was just a fact.

"No," I whispered, suddenly feeling a wave of unexpected emotions tearing through me.

Charlie nodded, already knowing what I was going to say before I opened my mouth again. Like I said, this wasn't really a surprise ending, but it didn't mean that either of us wanted to admit it either.

He finally placed the black velvet box on the table, still focused on it. He sighed and then reached out his hand, asking for mine in return. I wholly obliged, taking his warm invitation. I really did love this man sitting across the table from me. No matter what, I loved him.

Clutching my hand in his, Charlie said, "Emmie..."

I always got chills when he called me that. My mother had inevitably cursed me for life with the wicked name Esmerelda. Seriously, that was the name she put on my birth certificate and everything. She was a huge fan of the classics as well.

In school, the kids found new and unusual ways to punish me with nicknames so I wound up just telling people to call me Em. Anything sounded better than Esmerelda.

But the first time Charlie ever said my name it came out as Emmie, which sounded perfect, but any words coming out of those impeccable lips sounded amazing.

This time, that name just didn't feel right, it felt tainted.

"Emmie," he repeated again. "I am sorry for the way things have been for the past few months." He paused again, recalling our history, good and bad, once again. After a moment of silence, he smiled and said, "Do you remember that night we had the big thunderstorm?"

I smiled too, bigger than this moment should have granted. The bittersweet memory played through my mind as if it were yesterday. Still clutching his hand, I chuckled, "You got out of that car in the pouring rain, soaking your brand new wool sweater, just to open my door, and used your jacket to shield me from the rain." I smiled, seeing him in my mind, sopping wet, "You looked like a drowned rat, all just to be a gentleman."

Then, I remembered his three hundred dollar sweater that hung in my living room by the fireplace and how it had shrunk to a doll size. I felt so terrible for ruining something so valuable, but he could have cared less. We hadn't even noticed it until morning because as soon as we got out of the rain and warmed ourselves by the fire, clothes were the last thing on our minds for the rest of the evening.

"You wrapped us both up in my pink and green quilt and we watched the fire burn out." However, the fire between us only continued to burn all night long.

I had to stop myself, I was enjoying the memories a little too much for the moment.

"I didn't watch the fire. I couldn't take my eyes off of you." He had a pained smile on his angelic face as he looked down at my tiny hand perched in his strong fist. He stroked my palm with his fingers.

"That night..." Charlie continued, stumbling over every word. "I, I have never...been...happier in my...whole life." His last few words cracked and he cleared his throat.

Still rubbing my hand, only more forceful now, he continued. "Sometimes I think that if we had just stayed wrapped up in that blanket." He paused again, reminiscing. "Or if I had moved into your little cottage in the woods, instead of having you move here."

He shook his head as if New York City was disgusting to him at this moment. As if things would have been perfect between us in my hometown. I doubted it was the scenery.

Looking at him, his face became so distant and fragile, like a little boy who had just lost his puppy. "Maybe we would have been able to keep our fairy tale alive…"

I felt his hand slipping out of mine and I grabbed it up tighter than ever, not letting him go. "Don't you ever for one second think that I regret anything we have shared. That is not what I mean. I am a changed person because of you Charlie Cooper. You are such an amazing man and I love you so much."

With that, I burst into tears. I would be surprised if the last few words were even audible between sobs. Charlie climbed around the table and gathered me into his arms like he always used to. It was such a great feeling that I almost forgot where we were, and more embarrassingly, why we were there.

I drew my head back from his chest and looked him square in his smoldering eyes. They showed all of the same emotions that I was feeling, with one exception. I could see the finality in them. Almost like his heart had given everything up and I could see the inevitability hovering in his heartbreaking gaze.

I knew this was what had to be. It was the best thing for both of us, but the heart doesn't always enjoy doing what is best. And no matter how much our hearts were shattering into tiny shards, we couldn't chicken out now. We owed that much to each other.

I did my best to pull myself together and out of his intoxicating embrace. I might be able to do this, but I wouldn't be able to do it while wrapped in his arms. I looked at him, grabbed his face between both of my shaking hands and kissed him hard on those tender lips that I always found comfort in, knowing there would never be another kiss after this. I stayed locked on his lips for as long as my heart could manage, and then let my grip on him go.

There was no need for an actual goodbye, from either of us. Those words would have been daggers to the hearts that were already sliced open. We had said everything that needed to be said.

I slid my chair back from the table, mustered up the most pathetic smile I had ever smiled and stood up. His gentlemanly nature forced him out of his seat as well and he watched me walk out of the restaurant, and his life, forever. I never looked back, never looked around at all of the disgusted faces of the other restaurant patrons and staff. I just put one foot in front of the other and marched out of there as fast as I could without tripping over my own feet.

The rush of cold air that hit me when I threw open the door was like a thousand needles stinging my flushed cheeks. My tears, that I could no longer contain, were almost freezing in lines down my face. Luckily they didn't stop flowing long enough to actually freeze. I flagged down a taxi, being as Charlie had driven us to the restaurant, and I wasn't about to go back in there and ask for a ride home.

"Damn it!" I cried out loud. "Home…"

Chapter 2...

One of the most awkward breakups involves two people who are extremely in love with one another, smart enough to realize that they weren't meant to be, but only after they had decided to share their home.

After I left the restaurant and climbed into the cab that had so politely stopped (after about fifty others left me standing there on the corner sobbing, right in front of the scene of my crime) I was dumbfounded when the driver asked, "Where to Miss?"

I had no idea.

Of course I couldn't go home. My home, at the time, was Charlie's Fifth Avenue apartment, and that was the last place on Earth I could go.

I must have looked like a complete mess when I lifted my head up to look at the burly young man sitting on the other side of the glass partition. He caught my eyes with his and then quickly looked away, as if he could feel the intrusion in his glance. Was it possible that he could read my transgressions all over my face? Or perhaps he just saw a woman weeping and didn't want to get involved.

"Uh, its ok, you can just take your time and let me know when you're ready to go, alright lady?" His head was tilted down towards his steering wheel when he said it, not wanting to make eye contact again.

Normally in this city, as soon as your behind slid across the vinyl seat in the back of those yellow cars, the meter was running. I guess he felt pity on me because the only movement I saw from the front seat was his hand tugging on the worn Yankees cap clamped down on his head. He never once came close to reaching for that cash counting timer perched on his dashboard.

Finally, after a few long and silent moments, I courageously declared, "23rd and Canal in So Ho please."

It was the only address I knew, other than my own. Or I guess it is Charlie's now, not mine.

"Right away Miss," the man nodded his head in acknowledgement and peeled away from the curb. Perhaps he knew that I was fleeing.

One weekend last fall, when Charlie was out of town on business, I made the decision to venture out on my own and partake in the kind of culture that couldn't be found within the radius of Fifth Avenue. Nothing sultry, just a little more art savant than Wall Street had to offer.

I had been living in the city for quite a while, but hadn't seen much of New York at all. Charlie was very particular about me not going into any unkempt neighborhoods-especially if he was not accompanying me.

However, being an independent soul, I was never really comfortable listening to what other people told me I could or could not do. In fact, telling me I couldn't go somewhere made it the most appealing place in the world to me. I was definitely a descendent of Eve. I can feel her pain on the whole "apple" incident.

There just so happened to be a street fair in So Ho the weekend that Charlie was in Boston at a business conference. Of course, he knew nothing about my intentions of visiting such an obscure part of town. I took three separate trains to get there, getting off at the wrong stop twice and finally deciding to walk sixteen blocks toward some mariachi music and the unmistakable fragrance of meat on a stick.

I felt completely at home as soon as I turned the corner and saw the streets crowded with people, arts, crafts, music, dancing and food. Lots and lots of food. Back home, we would have street fairs every year in the fall. Everyone in town would come out, if not only for the delicious hometown cooking and familiar company, but because the fair was the most exciting thing that happened in a small town.

As I walked around, visiting each stand and getting reminiscent of home, I found myself being drawn to the sweet sounds of an acoustic guitar being delicately plucked in a hypnotic rhythm. It was like a siren's call to my soul. I forced my feet in the direction of the melody.

Tucked in between a gyro stand and a hemp lover's fantasy was a young man holding a beat up guitar, just sitting cross-legged on the curb. He was dressed very modestly, but with a style all his own – worn in blue jeans, a button down red and gray flannel with a hand-painted t-shirt underneath, a buckle bracelet around his taught wrist and shaggy chestnut hair that he kept flipping out of his eyes while he played.

To most city passerby's' he would've been mistaken for a homeless man playing on the streets for money, but here in this neighborhood, he looked almost magical. And the music that was emanating from his fingertips provided proof to that judgment.

I gazed at him for what seemed to be an eternity until the song was finished and he looked up at me while reaching for his bottle of water sitting between his crossed legs.

"Oh, hey, didn't know anyone was standin' there." His voice seemed a little startled, and I noticed immediately it was nothing like Charlie's. Charlie's voice was very deep and manly, while this man's voice was a little more high-pitched, like a younger boy, but nonetheless full of the same arrogance. Maybe that was just a man thing. He also looked a great deal younger than Charlie, closer to my own age, maybe twenty-one or twenty-two.

He tipped the water up to his mouth and chugged half the bottle in one gulp. Placing the guitar between his legs where his water had just been, he wiped the sweat off of his brow with his flannel sleeve. It took me a few moments to realize that I was still staring at him, with my mouth gaping wide open like a crocodile eyeing his prey. I quickly snapped my jaw shut before he could look at me again and cleared my throat.

"Ahem, uh, sorry. I didn't mean to stare, it's just that was the most beautiful song I have probably ever heard, and I didn't expect to hear it on a street corner in So Ho." My face immediately flushed crimson with embarrassment. My words were all true; I just didn't know why I had even said anything to him. It wasn't like me to talk to complete strangers sitting on street corners.

"Oh, well I usually sit here and play, just normally there isn't this much of a crowd. Didn't expect the fair, but who says I have to change my routine for them, right?" He raised his eyebrow at me and shot me a devastating half smile as he shrugged his shoulders and picked up his guitar again. He began plucking the strings with his fingertips, not playing anything in particular as far as I could tell, just messing around I suppose. Then he looked back at me and asked, "You play?"

Again, I blushed, "Oh no, no, not me! Well, I've played a little piano in my younger days, but…"

In my younger days? Really? I just said that? Who was I?

"Ah, you tickle the ivories huh? I was never able to pick that up myself. Me and The Gibson here have always had a calling for one another I guess."

"The Gibson?" I asked, completely oblivious to what he was talking about.

With a quiet chuckle, he pointed to the front of the guitar where it read, clear as day, Gibson in fancy lettering. There goes me playing it cool.

"Oh, yes, *the Gibson*. I get it." Yeah, there was absolutely nothing cool about me. "So, what was that song you were playing? Was that classic rock or something newer on the radio?"

Again, he smiled, but this time he looked down at his fingers as if he were embarrassed. "Uh, no. That's a Jackson Thomas original."

I didn't want to make the same mistake twice so I didn't ask who Jackson Thomas was. Probably some new rising star on the radio. I hardly ever listened to the radio. With having no car of my own and always being on the corporate schedule, there just wasn't an opportunity to listen to any music that wasn't played in an elevator or at a cocktail party.

"Well, you played it really well. I know he would be proud of your rendition." That should keep me in good graces.

To my chagrin, he laughed loudly now, almost spitting his water out onto the street. I had no idea what I said wrong.

After his snickering stopped, he put the guitar down on the ground and stood up. He brushed off his pants, outstretched his arm to mine and said, "Let me introduce myself. My name's Jackson Thomas." Then, he uncontrollably chuckled again.

Extremely red faced and now wishing I could crawl into the sewer vent beneath his feet, I reached my hand out to meet his and whispered, "I'm, um, Emmie."

"Ok, Um-Emmie, it's a pleasure to meet you." He gave me a funny glance, but then there was that smile again.

"It's just Emmie." I laughed awkwardly. "Is it ok to say that I feel like an idiot?"

"As long as you liked the song, *Emmie*, I don't care what you feel like."

"Oh, I absolutely loved it. That song, well, that song was just, oh! I have no words." The excitement was building in me just remembering the sweet melody. I was as giddy as a school girl. No, scratch that, a school girl who had just gotten a pony.

Jackson smiled, dragging his fingers through his unkempt hair and flung his guitar around his back.

"Well Emmie, I thank you for the words of encouragement. You are officially the first person to hear that song, so I am glad that you liked it. Most people around here just keep on walking when I play. And most times, that's what I'd rather them to do. But I'm glad you stopped."

It felt kind of like he was flirting with me, and I am not going to lie and say I didn't enjoy it. It had been awhile since a man even looked at me in a way that wasn't him thinking "Charlie's woman." Oh yeah, I had almost forgotten about Charlie. That's funny; he was usually the only thing on my mind.

"Oh yes, well, I should probably get going then. There's a lot to see around here today, isn't there?" I didn't want to offend him, but I also didn't feel comfortable flirting with another man while Charlie was out of town.

"Well, I do know the area. I can show you around, if you'd like?" He twirled his arm around into the street like a spokesperson to guide me.

"I have a boyfriend." I blurted out. The words sounded like they were coming from a thirteen year old girl. As soon as they came out I wished I could grab them out of the air and shove them back into my mouth. I hoped I hadn't offended him.

Again, Jackson chuckled. "Ok, well, I guess that means no then?" He kept on laughing as he turned to walk away. I don't know why he thought that was so funny, but he seemed to enjoy making me feel like a naïve teenager. He twirled back around on one leg towards where I was still standing and said, "Hey, uh, if it makes a difference, I have a girlfriend. I just thought you looked a little lost and maybe I could show you around." I guess I hadn't offended him as much as I thought if he was still willing to show me around.

Relieved, and again embarrassed for the third time today, I said, "Oh, ok then. I guess that would be nice. Well, as long as your girlfriend would be ok with it."

"I think we are in the clear." He giggled.

Perhaps I was being a little paranoid, but, other than Charlie, I had never spoken to a stranger on the street before and the only reason I didn't run screaming from Charlie was because he had me wrapped up in his arms at the time.

"I suppose I could use a little help. I don't even know where I was headed; I just wanted to go somewhere different. Somewhere other than Fifth Avenue."

Should I have told him I live on Fifth Avenue? What if he was a stalker or something? He seemed harmless enough, but isn't that how those scary movies started-some unsuspecting girl believing in the kindness of strangers?

"Well, this is definitely different. I'd just be careful though. There are a lot of *crazies* out here. It's a good thing you've got me to show you the difference between the eccentric's and the straight up nut jobs."

Ok, so I was the easiest person in the world to read. Was fear just written on my face?

Jackson continued, "There are plenty of things to see, but I was actually just getting ready to get a bite to eat. I mean, this place doesn't normally smell this good. Are you hungry, or doesn't your *boyfriend* let you eat?"

Now he was just teasing me. Wasn't it too soon for teasing? It was already starting to feel like we were old friends. Was that odd?

"Yes, I'm allowed to eat." I threw a frustrated glance at him. "What kind of food do they have?"

"Well, I can see that you are going to be very picky," (teasing again), "so let's start from the top. Ok, so you got your ethnic foods-gyro's you see of course, your everyday food – burgers, hotdogs, French fries. And then you've got your traditional "food on stick" options – corndogs, kabobs, caramel apples." He bowed his head down and looked at me straight in the eyes, awaiting my answer.

I showed no sign of enthusiasm, so he continued, "But...if you're wantin' something with a little more hometown feel, and you don't mind skipping right to the dessert, you've got the classic funnel cake, which is my personal favorite."

"Oh yes! Funnel cakes are my favorite too!"

"Funnel cake it is. I have to warn you though. I don't like to share so you'd better get your own."

"Oh, don't worry. I'm so hungry I could probably eat two!" My eyes were wide with anticipation.

"Is that a challenge? Oh, well, it's on then, little lady!"

He made a break for it, racing me to the stand and to my strange astonishment, I raced him right back. He seemed to really bring out this odd side of me that I didn't know existed. And I had only known him about ten minutes. It was rather freeing to not have to be as uptight and proper as I usually had to be around Charlie and his associates.

We got our funnel cakes, two a piece, and ate them while Jackson showed me around the rest of the small fair. There was so much culture and art to take in, so much more than I had seen in my time here.

I also learned that Jackson lived in an efficiency apartment located in an old warehouse just a few blocks from where we got corndogs after the two funnel cakes didn't fill me up. It seemed really odd to me that he basically lived in a warehouse, but I suppose for a musician and his artist girlfriend, it was the perfect fit. He actually had a day job working for a real estate firm downtown, but his passion was for his Gibson.

He told me a little about his girlfriend Amber, I think mostly to appease my trepidations about spending time alone with him. She was a sculptor who made very little money and relied on Jackson to support her dreams. They had been together only a few months before she moved her stuff into his apartment and he became her live in meal ticket. He just didn't seem to care enough to get rid of her. He said it was nice to have someone around to eat cereal with in the morning. I didn't disagree because, in a way, I felt like that about Charlie, even though I suppose I was getting a meal ticket of my own.

After an entire day wandering around the streets I had been so terrified of just this morning, the sun was setting and Jackson had to go.

He reached into his pocket and handed me a card with his address and phone number on it, since he mostly worked from home and said, "It has definitely been an interesting day Emmie. I am so very glad that you decided to stalk me today and allowed me to show you around."

"I wasn't stalking you! Your music was luring me. You really ought to watch that you know! Next time you won't meet someone as wonderful as me." I cocked my head and smiled at him. Was I flirting back? I had to stop myself! "Ok well I better get out of here before it gets dark."

"Yes, and tell that boyfriend of yours to let you out more. A caged bird goes a little wild if she doesn't see the light of day every once in a while." Again, he smiled that crooked smile at me.

"Well, it was very nice meeting you Jackson. Thank you for the tour, and the funnel cake race. Perhaps I will see you again soon?"

"I definitely hope so Emmie."

My face turned crimson as I crouched into the cab he had hailed for me. He told the driver where I needed to go. Apparently, he had the memory of an elephant since I only told him where I lived once and that was hours ago. He whipped out a fifty dollar bill and gave it to the cabbie before I could say anything and smacked the top of the cab to go. I made a face at him as I drove away and he waved back with a grin.

That was Jackson Thomas.

He was devious and cunning and nothing at all like Charlie. Charlie was a gentleman who always treated me like a princess, opened up doors and showered me with gifts and compliments.

Jackson teased me, got on my nerves and made me want to scream. And that is where I was headed at this very moment. I had nowhere else to go, and nowhere else I wanted to go. I needed him.

Chapter 3...

The part of town called So Ho, South of Houston or Lower Manhattan, wasn't on any map or tourist flyer I had ever read when I came to New York. Not saying it was insignificant; it just wasn't what most people came to New York to see. The big attractions are all located in New York City: Times Square, Grand Central Station, The Empire State Building, and Radio City Music Hall. These were what attracted people to the city. And for the romantics like me, there was always a casual stroll down Central Park.

But those days were far behind me. Now, as I looked out the window of this cab into the dark night, the bright city lights were fading as I entered the eccentric ambiance of the "Art District."

Jackson had shared with me a little bit of the history of how So Ho became what it is today. I snuck away again and stopped in to see him about a week after our carnival adventure when Charlie was on another Saturday client meeting. Amber was off scouting new ideas for her art so he took me on a long walk through town.

The actual story itself of So Ho's history wasn't the most interesting tale, but the way he spoke, he could have been reading a how-to book and it would have sounded like a sonnet.

"You see, there was a big industry boom back in the late 1800's, and the people started moving uptown." He stretched his hand across the skyline in the direction of uptown New York.

"These warehouses," pointing into the air at everything so I could almost visualize it happening right before my eyes, "were filled with fabric and china and glassware. You know, all that garbage they sell at department stores, places like that? Anyhow, so business was really booming at that time for the higher class stores. The more things were heating up down here, people got stir crazy."

"So, when the *upscale citizens*," he pointed his nose in the air and flicked his collar up, "decided to take their businesses uptown as well, what was left became a town full of sweat shops. It soon acquired the nickname *Hell's Hundred Acres*. Sweat shops…Hell…you get it right?"

I quickly shook my head, not wanting to interrupt his story.

He took a huge bite out of the pretzel we got from a street vendor who had only one hand but, as Jackson put it, *"could twirl out a piece of dough like nobody's business."* He continued, while chewing, "So, then Uncle Sam decides that maybe this isn't such a good idea having all of these sweat shops down here, and they posted new laws saying they'd have to close shop."

At this point, I was thoroughly intrigued by his story, or perhaps by the childlike quality he had in his eyes as he talked about his home town. He was born and raised in New York, just south of the Bronx. He had such a deep accent that sometimes I couldn't quite understand the words he said, and the pretzel jammed in his cheeks didn't help either.

He twirled around and guided me down a tight alley to get the full effect of his story. His voice got deep and gloomy. "So, the streets became a ghost town, dark, empty and filled with these huge vacant warehouses where no one was allowed to work." As we continued our walk, it got darker and more constricted in the alley. I was actually starting to get scared myself, but I had come to know that with Jackson, things were never really as dramatic as they seemed.

"With these empty places, naturally come squatters. These warehouses and lofts were the perfect refuge from the brisk winter nights and even with no electricity, the wind and the snow were kept out."

Just as we were creeping into the darkest part of the street, we rounded a corner and stepped back out into the bright sunlight. "And from that darkness, emerged hundreds of bright stars: painters, dressmakers, glassblowers, actors, and of course..." he said, clearing his throat and tapping on his chest, "musical genius's like me. It was magical and brilliant. What was once something so hellish had transformed into a beautiful epiphany." His eyes were so bright and animated thinking of all of the raw and amazing talent that had probably walked down these streets.

"So, that is why I love it here." He looked around with a large grin on his face, proud to be a part of this magical place. "Ya know, John Lennon loved So Ho too."

He teased me because he knew that I had previously given away my secret imaginary love affair with John Lennon. He was one of my favorite artists and being the romantic that I was, the story of John and Yoko was just one of the most amazing and tragic true life love stories of all time.

"He also loved to take long strolls in Central Park with the love of his life Yoko." I teased him right back. How dare he think he can test my knowledge of John Lennon.

"Huh, well, maybe you will have to take me for a stroll there sometime, just to, ya know, get a feel for the place-one artist to another. Maybe I can channel his untimely energy or something?'

He would always say things like that, things that made me unsure if he was flirting with me or just being silly. I felt both uncomfortable, and insanely intrigued by this extraordinary man.

Quickly changing the subject before I could get too flustered by his words, he got back to his story. "So, that is the history of So Ho, and all of its enchanting glory. It is both magical and utterly tragic at the same time. I guess you could say it is the "John and Yoko" of cities, turning something that people thought of as dreadful into the greatest love of all time, as you put it." He smiled his exquisite crooked smile in my direction and quickly turned away to take another bite of his pretzel.

We walked for hours that day, past all of the sights I was seeing fly by from my taxi window right now. For some reason, I couldn't stop thinking about him, but I was also scared to death.

What was I going to do when I saw him? I had no idea. He always told me I could stop by whenever I was in the area, but I don't think he meant in the middle of the night when I had just burned my last New York City bridge and had no place to stay.

I couldn't even give him a heads up, I was already on my way and what would I say? *"Oh hey Jack, it's Emmie.*

I just destroyed my relationship and am now officially homeless. Is it ok if I crash here for a while?"

I really wasn't cut out for living in a rational society filled with actual people. Perhaps I should move out west somewhere. Get myself a little cabin in the woods, make my own clothes, live off the land and have no contact with any other human being whatsoever. I seemed to just mess up every relationship I ever had. And being as I had only known Jackson for about 3 months now, I'm sure I would scare him away too; showing up on his doorstep like an orphaned baby.

"Miss, uh, we are here." The polite cab driver pointed out, after we had been parked for apparently a few moments. I came out of my mental coma and reached into my bag for some money.

As I pulled out my only $20, which I knew from previous rides was not even enough to get me half of where we had driven, he put his arm up and said, "Oh no, please, don't worry about it. I was going this way anyway."

"No, I really must pay you. I just thought I had more money. I wasn't expecting to…please, take it." I tried to push the bill into his hand.

"Ma'am, please don't take offense to this, but it looks like you might need that twenty dollars a little more than I do right now." He motioned to the empty purse where the twenty dollars sat all alone. "And besides, if I don't do one good deed a day, the big guy wouldn't be very happy with me." He pointed to the plastic Jesus figurine plastered on his dash.

Pitifully, I put the twenty back in my purse, knowing that he was probably right, and shook my head. "Thank you, you have no idea how you saved me."

"Glad to be of service, and I hope that whoever you are seeing treats ya' better than the last guy."

Not knowing what to say, and not wanting to argue with this kind man about how Charlie did nothing but give me kindness I didn't deserve, I climbed out of the cab and let him drive away.

I stood on the sidewalk, frozen to the cracked concrete. It was almost 10:30 pm, and most of the surrounding apartments looked like their inhabitants were already in bed for the evening. Again, this was nothing like New York City. People were out at all hours of the night. It was the place to be. This place, on the other hand, was almost reminiscent of its former "ghost town."

I mustered up the courage of the cowardly lion, enough to get my feet moving, but not enough to make them strong, and climbed the stairs to Jackson's loft. When I got to the top, I took a deep breath and pushed the buzzer for apartment 3. I waited for what seemed like an eternity, and heard nothing.

Oh great, he isn't home! Now what am I going to do? I doubt I will be able to find another cab around here at this hour, and even if I do, where will I go? I only have twenty dollars and that won't get me any further than the end of the block.

Just as I was ready to start hyperventilating and falling into a full blown panic attack, the buzzer rang back and the large metal door unlocked for me. Weird, do people around here normally let strangers inside without asking who it is first?

I wasn't about to look a gift horse in the mouth so I scooped open the door and all but ran inside. Jackson lived on the third floor, basically the "penthouse" of this old warehouse full of apartments, so I had quite a trek up the stairs, but that gave me a little time to compose myself before anyone saw me.

I got close to the top and realized that I had been staring at my feet the whole time I was climbing the stairs. When I lifted my head, I saw the friendly face I was so terrified and so excited to see, leaning against the wall in the stairwell outside of his apartment, watching me and chuckling to himself.

"Hey there."

"Hey." I barely breathed out. That was all I had to say.

He swung open the door and let me inside without another word. I walked into his absolutely amazing loft, still dressed in my little black dress that I had so long ago put on for a completely different reason altogether, and waited for him to follow me. He was right behind me, closing the door and strolling past me to the kitchen.

His loft was incredible. I had never actually been inside, only to the door and took a peek once or twice. It was a completely open space with twenty foot high ceilings, exposed steel beams and art everywhere.

His girlfriend Amber was, as he had mentioned the first time I met him, a sculptor who dabbled in very strange art choices. However, he never told me that she painted and I found myself surrounded by the most beautiful paintings hung on every wall.

This wasn't the kind of art that you would find in Charlie's apartment. It was very colorful, very abstract and wasn't likely to be found in a department store.

"Oh so Amber took up painting did she?" I was hoping to deflect his attention from why I was standing here in his living room at such a late hour.

"Uh, no, not really." He looked down at his feet as his face turned crimson. "Just another thing I was trying my hand at."

He stared at me, propped up against the bar in the kitchen. "I am forever a work in progress, but if I am going to live up to John Lennon status, I gotta work harder." He smiled again, still watching me like a hawk. I looked back at him and finally noticed that he was wearing what looked to be pajamas. I had woken him and Amber up.

"Oh Jack, I am so very sorry, I woke you both up. Amber is probably fuming, wondering why some strange girl is busting into your apartment in the middle of the night like this. I'm so embarrassed."

"Slow down, you didn't wake me up. And it's not the middle of the night, it's barely eleven. I am the one who should be apologizing for allowing you to see that my social life has declined to sitting home alone on a Friday night."

"Alone? So Amber isn't here, oh good. No, I don't mean good like good I'm glad she isn't here, but good I'm glad I didn't wake her. I haven't even met her yet, I don't want to be making enemies before we even meet." I was rambling, and he was enjoying my nervousness. He laughed out loud at me.

"Well, I wouldn't worry about that so much."

"No, I always make a bad impression. I'm sorry, I really should go." I took a step for the door, but stopped, realizing the reason I was here in the first place. I had nowhere else to go.

"No, I meant, I wouldn't worry about that because Amber is no longer a worry. We decided to go our separate ways last week."

"Oh, oh…I'm sorry. I had no idea. Well, of course I had no idea, I haven't talked to you in a couple weeks and then here I am just bombarding you like this."

"Calm down Emmie, take a deep breath, you're going to hyperventilate." He was again laughing. He always seemed to get a kick out of my craziness.

He left his perch in the kitchen and came over to me, leading me to sit down on the red overstuffed couch in the middle of the living area. He flopped himself down in the recliner that was next to it and continued to stare at me, not saying anything. I suppose he was waiting for me to do or say something.

"Well, I guess you are wondering what I am doing here, right?"

"No, I wasn't actually. I tend not to question when a beautiful woman in a tight black dress comes a knockin' on my door." There were those pearly whites again.

I immediately flushed red. And I couldn't hide it, my entire face down to my exposed shoulder blades were crimson. Other than being embarrassed, I think I was flattered. After assuming I looked like a train wreck from my previous endeavors this evening, it felt good to get a compliment, especially one from him. He rarely seemed to compliment, mostly he just teased.

He was still silent and staring at me. I looked around the apartment again, taking it all in and trying to avoid his watchful gaze. It had such an interesting smell, like cinnamon and musk.

I hadn't really taken notice of many smells lately. Nothing in New York had smelled all that pleasant since I had been here, with the exception of the coffee shops that I never went into. I tried to contain my sense of smell while I was here; sewers are around every corner you know.

"So, you really painted all of these?" I asked, pointing to the tremendous works of art all around the room.

He eased back into the chair, "Uh, yeah, I know, don't quit my day job. I was just messing around with paint." He sounded like he was embarrassed. There was clearly no reason to be anything other than proud.

"Oh no, no no no! These are so great! You have more talent in your little finger than I have in my entire body." I was always utterly amazed at the things he could do.

"I don't believe that for one second." He leaned back up in his chair, getting closer to me. "So, as to why you picked such an odd hour for a friendly visit...?"

I still wasn't sure what I would say to that question. Guess time was up for thinking.

"Uh, well Jack, you see..." I had nothing. All I could do was take a deep breath and sigh.

He raised one eyebrow in my direction. "One of those nights huh?"

"Yeah."

"Well, I am glad you are here regardless. You can help me with what I was working on." He shot up out of the recliner and grabbed my arm, pulling me off the couch.

"No, you don't understand, I am not being modest here. I am no good at painting..."

"I wasn't painting tonight. I was, hmm, well, I'm almost embarrassed to admit it..." He stopped in his tracks.

"You? Embarrassed? Never!" I teased him back. I was already feeling more comfortable here.

"Ok, well, I was trying my hand at something new this time. *Jack* of all trades if you will. The name suits so I gotta do Mommy proud." He smiled, shrugged his shoulders, and led me into the kitchen. I hadn't noticed, being blinded by the art and furniture and everything else that was so wonderful in this apartment. His kitchen was a mess. There were bowls and pans and flour   everywhere.

"You decided to become a tornado?"

"Ha, she makes jokes too! I gotta say, you've got more talent than you think little lady. No, I wanted to make a cake. It's not quite a manly thing to do, but I've got a hankerin for some fresh chocolate cake and since there isn't a twenty four hour bakery around, I thought, I can do that."

Chocolate cake reminded me of the dessert that Charlie and I were just about to share before he got down on his knee in the Italian restaurant. It was this amazingly decadent chocolate torte with drizzled raspberry sauce and whipped cream. It was my favorite treat, but now it would forever remind me of this wretched evening.

"Baking I can do! So, chocolate cake, ok, well, where's the box?"

"Boxes are for amateurs Emmie. What do you think I am? I am a "from scratch" kind of guy."

He proceeded to show me all of his raw ingredients and the recipe that looked like it was about a hundred years old.

He handed it to me and said, "Be careful with this. It was my great grandmother's and it is quite honestly the best chocolate cake you could ever imagine. However, it seems as though I don't have the same magical touch as she had. I can't seem to get it right. But I think I know what the problem is." He reached around me to get a wrapper that was on the counter behind my back.

"Unsweetened chocolate! Who buys unsweetened chocolate? Well, I know who bought it, me, but really, it shouldn't even exist!" He made a face as if he was disgusted with himself for even picking up the package.

"Well, some things call for unsweet..."

"No, no!" he interrupted me. "Nothing should ever call for unsweetened chocolate. What is that?? Chocolate can be anything-delicious, decadent, but never unsweetened!"

"I agree." What else could I do but agree. He was on a tirade about chocolate and arguing with him seemed futile.

"Ok, so I have a couple candy bars in the freezer. I think that will work, but you can be the judge." He reached into the frosty mist and pulled out half a dozen chocolate bars. I was both envious and slightly aroused that he had so many candy bars just sitting in his freezer. It was every lonely woman's fantasy, or maybe just mine.

"Um, I don't know if these will work. They have peanut butter and caramel in them."

"I don't really see what you're getting at. What's wrong with peanut butter and caramel? Won't that just make it that much better?"

Again, I couldn't disagree.

I rolled up my sleeves and got to work, helping him gather all of the ingredients and melting down the frozen candy bars to add to our concoction.

We didn't say much while we were working, but every now and then he would look at me with a big grin on his face as I worked the kitchen.

It felt good to be able to bake again. I hadn't touched the stove in Charlie's apartment since the first week I was there and made a pot of tea. We always ate our meals at restaurants or parties. Once I had a plan to surprise him with breakfast, but I woke up to an empty bed due to one of his many early morning meetings.

"So, Emmie, where did you learn how to cook?" he said, sounding a little impressed by me this time. I wasn't used to that either.

"My mom was the most amazing cook. She always had elaborate meals for us growing up and I was lucky enough to be the only girl in a house full of boys. So I got to be the cook and my three brothers were my taste testers."

That's funny. I don't think Charlie even knew that about me. Huh.

"Three brothers? Wow, I guess that makes sense."

"What makes sense?"

"Well, it just gives me an idea of where you got your spirit from, that's all."

"My *spirit?* What does that mean?" I scowled at him. I couldn't help but feel a little offended.

"Oh don't get your panties in a twist, well, on second thought…" He tilted his head to the side and looked down at my dress.

"Excuse me, we are working here!"

He looked into my eyes, grinning wildly. Then he turned around to stir the pot of bubbling chocolate goo on the stove. "I just meant that you have this free spirit deep inside of you, screaming to get out, but you hide it underneath these layers of politeness and education. I always thought it was from your Manhattan boyfriend suppressing your every desire, but maybe it was hard to be yourself in a house full of men."

I forgot that I hadn't told him the details about my breakup with Charlie yet.

"Well, I wouldn't say a house full of *men*. Sometimes I really thought I was living at the zoo in the monkey pen."

Jackson put his spoon down and laughed out loud. "I'll tell ya what Emmie. You've gotta come over here at night more often. You aren't this funny during the day! But I forgot, your boyfriend probably wouldn't allow it." He rolled his eyes playfully.

"Speaking of, why are you allowed to be here tonight? Is he out of town again? Boy, I don't know that I would trust leaving you home alone so much. Some dastardly character like me might just take advantage of an unsuspecting beautiful woman like you." He dipped the spoon into the chocolate and took a taste.

"OW! Damn, that is hot. I think I burned my tongue!"

"Usually when chocolate is bubbling, it means it's pretty hot." I couldn't help but laugh at him now, flailing about the kitchen with his tongue sticking out. I grabbed a rag and ran it under cold water. I opened up my bag and grabbed a small brown bottle that I had put in there about a year ago. I poured some of the contents onto the rag and handed it to him.

"Here, put this in your mouth."

"Yeah, right. What is that?"

"Just trust me, put it in your mouth." I heard my mother's voice come out of my lips and cringed a little. That is exactly what she always told me to do when I burned my tongue.

Unwilling, Jackson shoved the rag into his mouth and his face changed from a scowl to a smile almost immediately.

Talking through the rag and barely making audible words, he said, "Rwowl, vat izz arraaazing! Vwot izz vat??"

I clasped my hand over my mouth to cover the burst of laugher that was about to escape, but it didn't help. He looked so funny standing there with the rag hanging out of his mouth, trying to be serious.

"It is lavender oil. My mom always had it close by when she was baking. It isn't the tastiest thing in the world, but it will soothe a burn in a matter of seconds."

"Ro, yreah" he mumbled.

I grabbed the towel from his jaw and smiled at him. "You don't have to keep it in there forever."

"Wow, I can't believe how quick that worked! You aren't some kind of witch are you?"

I shook my head no.

"Voodoo doctor?"

"Wrong again."

"Well, again I find myself grateful for knowing you. I just hope I will be able to taste our delicious cake when it is done. Are you ready for my hazardous chocolate mixture yet?"

"Yup, you can pour it right in here," I angled the blue glass bowl that was filled with the dry ingredients I just gathered together towards him. He grabbed the pot off the stove and carefully poured in the bubbling mixture. I stirred it into the rest of the ingredients and it formed a dark brown batter that I poured into the pan he had waiting for me. As I slid it into the oven, Jackson brushed off his flour covered pants and crossed his arms across his chest.

"Job well done! And only one of us got hurt. So, Emmie, are you ready to tell me why you are here?"

Chapter 4...

Beep beep beep! The timer on the stove alerted us that the cake was done. My tears were still fresh on my cheeks from telling Jackson about my horrible evening. I got up to turn it off and before I got past the couch, I found myself wrapped up in the arms of the man I had just bared my soul to. It was surprisingly heavenly.

He smelled absolutely amazing, even better than the chocolate cake aroma wafting through his entire apartment.

It's funny how a smell can affect you so much. His smell, the smell of musk and whatever cologne he was wearing, was going straight to my head-as if I wasn't already reeling.

We had never been this close before, never even touched, unless you count our hands grazing when we both reached for our funnel cakes on our first day together. It was such a strange, but very passionate feeling. Tingles were racing up and down my spine and I could barely breathe, even though he held me ever so gently.

One of his hands was clenched around my back and the other was cupping my head and stroking my hair. It was the most loving embrace I had ever felt, and he was practically a stranger to me. Yet, it felt perfect.

I lingered in his arms while the oven kept buzzing. We were coming desperately close to ruining another chocolate cake (if you count the three he made before I burst in on him), and he made no notion of moving. He was a fair amount taller than me, so my head was pressed tight to his chest and I could feel his heart beating against it. It seemed to be racing, but perhaps that was a combination of his and mine. I relaxed into his warm embrace and held him close.

After a few silent moments, he released me and slowly pulled back from my body. He lifted my chin up to face him and stared into my soggy eyes. It felt as if my heart would flutter right out of my chest. What was this I was feeling?

Before I could delve too deeply into it, he nodded his head and quickly peeled out of my arms. He left me standing there while he ran to the kitchen, grabbed a towel and pulled the cake out of the oven. I wasn't sure if I should have followed him, so I just stood there in his living room. I felt a little dejected, although I shouldn't have felt anything, we were just friends right?

"With all the work you put into this, I didn't want to ruin it before we had a chance to enjoy it... together." He said, smiling as he placed it on the counter to cool off.

I didn't say anything back. I had no words for what I was feeling. He didn't hesitate to exit the kitchen and resume his place next to me, but he just stood there too, staring into my eyes. He had an odd look on his face, not quite smiling, as if he was plotting his next move. Then, without telling me what he was doing, he walked back into the bedroom.

At first, I was thinking, *who does he think he is? I'm not going into the bedroom with him!* But then I saw him come right back out, a blue plaid blanket tucked under his arm.

Still not letting me in on his new plan, he came over to me, grabbed my hand and led me to the kitchen. He grabbed the pan with the arm that was holding the blanket, slid two forks between his lips, since he didn't have a free hand (and he wasn't letting mine out of his grasp) and led me out the door.

Right outside his apartment were stairs that went up. I thought he told me his apartment was on the top floor.

"Where are we…?" I barely spit out the words before getting *shushed* through the metal forks between his teeth. He continued to pull me up the stairs until we reached a door that said "Roof Access" on it. He plowed through the door with his full arm and pulled me along with him.

The night sky was very clear and there were too many stars to count. The moonlight lit up the rooftop, glistening off of the rusty exhaust pipes and vents that we were weaving in and out of. Around one very large metal obstacle, he guided me to a clearing where I could see a small bench.

He nodded his head, gesturing me to sit down, his teeth still clenching the set of forks as he let his warm palm drop from mine. I hesitantly sat down on the cool bench, never taking my eyes off of him and silently wishing he wouldn't have let go.

The evening chill was already creeping into me but he wrapped the blue blanket around my shoulders and I was instantly engulfed in his delicious aroma again. I leaned my head into the soft cotton throw, inhaling it completely.

Had he not been busy, he perhaps would have thought me a little crazy for sniffing his blanket. However, if he didn't realize I was crazy by now, being privy to all of my foolish antics, I was most likely in the clear. Or perhaps he liked crazy.

He emptied his arms of the cake and silverware. Then he turned to me, smiled and said "Ok, so, now is the true test," as he handed me one of the forks.

I didn't move, just stared at him like I had been doing this whole time and he nudged me, "Aw, come on, I had to taste the last three! Now it's your turn to be the guinea pig."

So, I cautiously stuck my fork into the dark brown mound that he had placed on the bench beside me and slowly popped it into my mouth.

"Oh…my…God." That was all I could manage to say through the cake melting inside of my mouth.

"That bad huh?"

"Um, no." As usual, Jackson had managed to treat me with something that was beyond amazing. His music, his art, and now, his chocolate cake. I stuck my fork in again for another bite.

"Ok, don't eat it all now! I'd like to try some of your handiwork." He teased and stuck his fork in the other side of the pan.

As I chewed my second bite of the most heavenly chocolate cake I'd ever tasted, I looked up at the stars. It was such a beautiful night. Funny, I wouldn't have said that a few hours ago. I snuggled into the blanket some more and relaxed into the bench.

"Wow! That is good. I've gotta get your recipe. Oh that's right, I did this, with a little help of course." Jackson laughed, but this time it was more subtle, less teasing in his tone. He sat down on the bench next to me and watched me enjoying his great grandmother's dessert.

"I can't believe how clear the sky is. I could have sworn it was sleeting earlier. But now, there is not a cloud in the sky. Crazy how the weather can change like that. You go through a storm, just to see the most beautiful rainbow on the other side." He turned to stretch his legs out on the tin roof and arched back, putting his hands behind his head.

"So, I guess it goes without saying that you need a place to sleep tonight?"

I froze, my fork sticking out of my mouth. Without turning my head, my eyes left the night sky to rest on his face. He was only looking at me from the corner of his eye, his head still cocked to the stars. I sighed and nodded my head.

"Well, it's a good thing I brought this blanket. It's gonna get cold tonight and I wouldn't want you to freeze up here while I am warm and toasty in my bed. It just wouldn't be right."

Part of me knew he was joking, but the other part of me wasn't quite sure and my fulfilled gaze turned into a frown.

"Oh Emmie,really? Do you think I am serious? Geez! I thought you knew me better than that! I would at least have the decency to bring you a pillow too."

Without hesitating, I backhanded him across the chest and his entire body folded in half. He started laughing out loud and he popped another bite of cake into his chuckling mouth.

After we had devoured about half of the delicious dessert, without one more word spoken between us, we simultaneously dropped our forks into the pan, admitting defeat. The cake had won, but I was sure there would be a rematch in the near future.

"Uh," he groaned, "Now, *that*, was good."

"Yes, it was perfect, thank you." There was a cold breeze up on the roof and without the warmth of the chocolate cake, I began to shiver.

"Are you cold? We should probably head back inside. I'm sorry."

"No, I'm fine. You must be freezing though, I'm hogging the blanket. Here." I said, pulling the cover off of my shoulder and handing it to him.

"Nah, I'm fine. I mean, don't get me wrong, I'd love to share that extremely tiny blanket with you, but perhaps we should go inside. I'd like to show you something anyway."

"Oh, ok." I pulled the blanket over my shoulder and snuggled back inside of it as we walked to the access door. He politely held it open for me; that was a first for him. Normally he was the first one in and I would have to watch so it didn't smack me in the face on my way through it.

When we got down to his apartment, he led me to the couch and told me to have a seat. He went back into the bedroom as he had before and was in there longer than it took him to get the blanket. I was anxious as to what he had for me. And wondering why he had anything for me in the first place.

He came back, carrying his guitar over his back. He sat down on the recliner and straddled the ottoman while he set up his guitar in his arms.

"Since you liked my song so much, I thought I would show you the finished product."

I was unexplainably excited and nervous at the same time. What I had heard before I loved, and I wasn't afraid of the song being bad. I was afraid of the feelings it would bring out in me. I had already cried on his shoulder once tonight, I really didn't want to do it again.

He plucked the strings once or twice and twisted the knobs to make sure it was in tune. I don't think I would have had any idea if it wasn't, but he would. He stared down at his fingers while he was tuning, but then he stopped and looked up at me.

"Now, you can tell me if you don't like it. Just know that your opinion is gauging whether or not you have a place to sleep tonight." He smiled and looked back down.

"Well, how much would I have to like it to get a bed to sleep in?" I couldn't believe I just said that. That really wasn't like me.

"Ha! That's more like it. See, you're starting to loosen up. I think I am a good influence on you Em." He never looked back up, just chuckled to himself and started in with his song.

His fingers carefully strummed the melody and he closed his eyes as he started to sing.

"The morning wind blowing in your hair,

Makes me smile when you aren't there,

I watch you quietly from afar

I wish that I was where you are

I miss your smile; I miss your embrace,

I wonder when I will see your face

How can you take my breath from me

When I used to breathe so easily?

Can I ever really exist

Without the sweetest taste of your kiss?"

I watched him play, and it was a completely different experience than it was the first time. I felt these emotions running through me, not just enjoying the song, but feeling it deep in my bones. Every word took on a new meaning to me and it felt like he was singing them to my soul.

I clung to every note that danced out of his mouth. I had never had anyone serenade me and now I understood what all of those cheesy romantic movies were trying to explain. I had no idea what or who it was about, and I was a fool to think that he had written this song for *me*, but I pretended nonetheless.

When he was in the middle of a guitar solo, he looked up at me and caught my eyes in a locked embrace. I couldn't look away, even though I could feel my face getting hotter to the point that he was probably staring at a tomato.

His eyes were piercing and although his fingers never stopped, it felt as though his mind wasn't just singing the song anymore. When it came time for him to sing again, he shut his eyes and freed me from his penetrating glance.

> *"Beautiful and powerful girl*
> *You put my heart in a whirl*
> *Inducing madness within my soul*
> *You make me want to lose control*
> *I feel alive when I'm with you*
> *I only hope you feel it too"*

At this point, my whole body was tingling. I hadn't felt the tingles in a very long time. Jackson made me feel the tingles whenever I was around him.

The weird thing was, it wasn't fairy tale perfect like it always seemed to be with Charlie. Things with Jackson were never perfect. They were messy and un-polite and filled with burned chocolate cakes and storm clouds. But in the midst of all of that, there were the rainbows. Even during the storm, there were rainbows. I didn't have to wait for the ebb and flow; behind every idiosyncrasy, were the rainbows.

Engulfed in my own emotions and trying to rationalize everything, the song was slowing down and the last string was strummed. He slowly pulled his head up as he rested the guitar on his lap. I could see that his face was nervous, awaiting my reaction. The question was, would I be able to give it to him?

We were left in a long silence after the music stopped. Both of us just sat there on baited breath, for two separate reasons. I wasn't quite sure what to say, but the thing I had going for me was that I wasn't looking at his face. My eyes were cast downward to his guitar, so I could sit here as long as I wanted to without saying anything. He couldn't trap me with his eyes unless I looked up.

"Ahem..." he cleared his throat. Guess I wasn't getting off that easily.

I lifted my head and was immediately bombarded by his glare. I still didn't know what I was going to say, but I opened my mouth anyway and let the words come to me.

"Wow." I didn't say there were a lot of words.

"Wow?"

"Yeah, wow."

"Um, Emmie, I know I said the roof over your head depended on your answer, but you know I was just kidding right? You don't have to worry, just give it to me straight." His words seemed in jest, but his tone was unfamiliar.

Normally he would have a smug attitude lingering behind every phrase, but this time he actually seemed genuinely worried that I wasn't going to like his song. I had to explain to him that he need not worry about that.

"Jack, I only have wow to say because it was phenomenal. I absolutely loved it, and no, I'm not just saying that because my room and board depends on it. I was moved by your song."

"That's funny, I didn't see you budge one inch." He smiled. There it was, that spunk. "And who said anything about *board.* I just promised a room." And there was that crooked smile again.

He started strumming again, but he wasn't playing, more like avoiding my glare. The tables had swiftly turned and it seemed as though he was the one under scrutiny now.

"Well, it is getting pretty late, and I wouldn't be a gentleman if I didn't offer you full use of my bed, which means I will need to be kicking you off of the couch so I can get some shut eye."

"Oh no Jack, I really couldn't kick you out of your bed. Please, let me take the couch. I am imposing on you enough already."

"Emmie, just the fact that you are here, safe and warm, means I could sleep on the floor and be comfortable. So, please, let me do the right thing and give you the bed. I spent an entire month's salary on that pillow top contoured thing, so I know it is much more comfortable than this hand-me-down couch."

I didn't want to tell him that this "hand me down" couch reminded me of my very similar secondhand couch I loved sleeping on in my cottage at home. I didn't want to tell him that because he had already heard enough of my sob stories tonight. He was being so kind, letting me stay, not to mention giving up his bed for me. I didn't want to offend him.

"Well, I have another favor to ask you." I shyly said, remembering that I had absolutely nothing along with me, and figuring it would be extremely difficult sleeping in this tiny black dress. I looked down and pulled at the black lace on the bottom.

"I've got an old t-shirt on the dresser. It's fairly large so you would probably be pretty comfortable in it. Unfortunately, I haven't gotten a chance to do laundry in a while so it's that or the suit I wore to communion when I was fifteen, although I'm pretty sure you want something more casual. Plus, that might also bring up some pretty confusing feelings for me seeing you in that."

He laughed as he ran his fingers through his unkempt hair and pointed towards the room.

"The bathroom is in there so feel free to freshen up or do whatever it is that girl's do to get ready for bed. It always astonished me that girls actually *get ready* for bed. I mean, why you can't just go to sleep is beyond me, but hey, the whole beauty sleep thing seems to work for you."

"Thanks Jack."

"Have I told you that I like you calling me Jack? You've never done that before tonight. I wonder why that is?"

"Oh, I don't know, sorry."

"No, I just said I liked it. You really gotta stop apologizing."

"Sorry, oh, oops. Guess that's a habit I've gotta work on."

"Well Emmie, you really turned my night around tonight. Here I was, stuck without a decent chocolate cake, waiting for the rain to come, and you brought me a rainbow."

I turned and walked into the room before he could see the huge grin brimming on my face. I felt very awkward being in his room, and being in his room *alone*, but I don't think I was ready to be in his room *with him*.

I looked around in the dark, searching for a light switch or a lamp, something to light my way. My hands were dragging on the walls until I felt a switch and turned it on. The light wasn't bright, and I think it was on a dimmer, but it was just enough to see how captivating his room was.

There was color on every wall. It was like one of those paint spinners you used to find at carnivals where you would spin the paper and when you squirted the paint on, it would twirl around into all of these magical swirls. Looking closer, I could see that in every swirl of paint were excruciatingly beautiful details-faces and hands and feet and flowers. Each had its own place, its own meaning and all of them breathtaking.

I wondered how he could even sleep, or if he ever did sleep, in this room. I traced my fingers all around every wall, stopping to gaze at all of the beauty around me. I lingered on one in particular, a beautiful girl, lying half naked and wrapped up in an orchid.

Next to the girl were two words scribed into one of the leaves of the flower: induces madness. I remember that was one of the lines in his song. I thought that phrase was weird, but seeing it on the wall in this way, I think I understood.

I reached the dresser; a vintage antique scrolled with intricate detailing and rubbed clean through some parts of the decades of paint layers. On top, I saw the t-shirt that Jackson meant for me to wear. It was very worn-in and larger than my whole body. I held it up to my chest and it came down to past my knees. As I held it close, I could smell him again and I pushed it against my face to breathe him in once more.

What had happened tonight? The series of events were trickling through my mind. No one could have guessed at the beginning of this night, when I put on this little black dress in the middle of my dressing room at Charlie's that I would be taking it off in Jackson's apartment. Well, not *taking it off* taking it off, but the way things had panned out was beyond comprehension.

It was supposed to be a typical Friday night: going out to a fancy restaurant, eating the same expensive food, drinking the same bottle of wine, driving home, putting on my fancy silk pajamas and going to bed on the opposite side of the bed as Charlie.

Now, I was putting on clothes that weren't mine and sleeping alone in a strange man's bed while he tried to sleep out on the couch in his living room.

And Jackson. *Jack.* What was this all about? I had just broken my heart, and Charlie's for that matter, and now I was thinking about another man? I was glad that Jackson had been a gentleman. The way my mind and body were acting this evening I wouldn't have trusted myself to do the right thing. And my conscience was telling me that the right thing was to sleep alone in this bed and let Jackson sleep out on the couch.

I slid off my dress and threw the oversized t-shirt over my head. Again, the smell of Jackson wafted to my nostrils. How could someone smell so amazing?

I pulled back the covers and climbed into his king size empty bed. I barely took up a fourth of it, and I thought about Jackson trying to fit his body on the tiny couch all night. Fighting the urge to get up and tell him to come join me, I ultimately decided that I needed to sleep alone tonight.

And with that thought, I remembered how utterly alone I really was. The whole ordeal with Charlie was finally starting to sink in and the tears were swelling up in my eyes as I laid there in another man's bed. I tried as best I could to hold in the loud sobs that wanted to come out. The last thing I needed was for Jackson to hear me. I had to suffer in silence tonight.

Chapter 5...

"Knock knock!" Jackson's voice was booming through the door. "Are we decent?"

I peeled the covers off of my face that had sometime throughout the night become lodged between the pillow and the mattress.

"Oh, yeah, I'm decent." Decent, yes, although I was afraid of what I must have looked like at that point. I was not one of those lucky girls that woke up beautiful. It was a good day if I woke up looking better than the bride of Frankenstein.

I heard the door knob turning and jolted upright in bed. With the few seconds I had, I tried to smooth myself out from the night of restless sleep I had just been awakened from.

I could immediately smell coffee, and hoped I wasn't going to have to force it down out of politeness.

"Wow, I guess I should have given you a moment." He snickered as he came towards me with a tray of food. "I can come back." He motioned towards the door with a huge grin on his face.

What *did* I look like?

My face flushed as I jumped out of bed, forgetting that I only had a shirt on and ran to the mirror on his wall. I looked rather decent for having slept all night. What was he talking about? I flashed him a questioning look.

"Oh really Emmie, you have got to learn how to read my sarcasm. You look beautiful. Now come on over here, get back into my bed," (he seemed to smile a little bigger when he said *my* bed), "so I can do the gentlemanly thing and give you breakfast in bed."

I suddenly realized that I was practically half naked standing in front of him so I ran back into the bed, as he had ordered, and pulled the covers up over my exposed legs.

"You really didn't have to do all of this. I mean, I am completely imposing upon you Jack."

Spread out before me on the tray were two hearty looking bagels, strawberry cream cheese, a sprinkle covered chocolate donut, apples, strawberries, grapes and some sort of fast food wrapped sandwich, along with a mug of steaming hot coffee and a glass of chocolate milk.

Seeing my eyes panning the tray, he quickly grabbed the fast food sandwich, "Not so fast! This one is mine. Normally I wouldn't have breakfast, but the place down the street makes the best egg and sausage sandwiches and I figured since I was going there for something for you, I'd get myself something."

"So, you think I would rather have healthy food than a sausage sandwich?" I smiled at him, eyeing the greasy sandwich in his hands.

"Oh, well I wasn't quite sure, but I remember you telling me how much you loved the bagels at that place, so that is what you get! And," he said, climbing onto the bed next to me and chomping down on his sandwich while continuing to talk with a mouth full of sausage and egg, "since I also remember you telling me you hate coffee, the only other drink they had was chocolate milk. I figured you would like it, considering that sweet tooth of yours."

"Boy, you really seem to remember a lot about me." I threw a questioning glance his way. "You aren't stalking me are you?" I joked, grabbing the bagel and smearing it with cream cheese.

"I believe you were the one knocking on my door last night."

Oh yeah, I kept forgetting why I was here.

Seeing my changed expression, Jackson quickly changed the subject. "So, since it is 10:00 am and you have yet to get out of bed, I suppose you don't have plans for the day?" he asked, shoving the last bit of his breakfast into his mouth and wiping his hands off on the crumpled jeans he was wearing. He must have slept all night in those uncomfortable clothes.

"Well, I was supposed to meet Char..." I stopped myself from saying his name. I would have to stop myself a lot. He was embedded in me like a tattoo. Not that I *had* a tattoo. That was something I was always afraid to do, but I imagine Charlie would be just as hard to get out of my skin.

"Ok, so no plans then? Great! I've got something that I have to show you." He was really good at judging when he needed to change the subject.

He jumped off of the bed, almost flipping the tray that was sitting between us and went over to his closet.

"You will probably need some clothes. I doubt you want to go traipsing around town in that t-shirt, or your black dress."

"I do have clothes you know." Not that I was ready to go get them. I was terrified to even think about going back there. What did I think; I could just never see him again? I lived there, my whole life was there. "I guess I have to eventually get my stuff…"

I started having a mini panic attack. What was I going to do? How could I go back there? What would I say? What if he already had someone else there? Suddenly I couldn't breathe.

"Yes, *eventually*. But today really isn't the day for that, now is it? So, you can borrow something of mine and we will worry about all of that later." He rummaged through his closet full of men's clothes, finding nothing that would remotely fit me.

"Hmmm…" he started to open a box that was on the floor of his closet and pulled out a few things that I hoped were not his.

"Why Jackson, I never knew you liked to dress up like a woman." I joked.

"Ha, Emmie, just when I think you completely lost your sense of humor. No, these are Amber's things. Today wasn't the day for her either. I will probably just have to send these things to Goodwill or something. I doubt she will be back for a couple pair of jeans and some tank tops."

He held a few items up. Amber was very different from me. Very thin and apparently very carefree about her body from the looks of the scantily covering clothing he was rummaging through.

"I don't suppose you would be comfortable in this, would you?" He held up a shirt between his two pinky fingers that was cut open on all sides and looked like moths had gotten to it in the box. I looked at it, and then looked down at my body with a bit of terror. He didn't really think…

"No, I suppose not. I don't even know which end is up on this thing." He fumbled with the torn fabric and threw it back in the box. Climbing back to his feet, he grabbed a sweatshirt from the hangers in front of him and onto the bed.

"That works. Like I said, we can worry about clothes later. I'd be ok if you just walked around in that t-shirt all day, but I think you might be a little cold."

He left the room so that I could get dressed, but not before making another comment about me being in his bed. I swear, I could never tell if he was serious or if he just really liked making me blush.

His sweatshirt smelled just like the t-shirt had last night and I held it up over my head for a few moments to linger in his scent. The jeans he gave me were a little snug but it seemed to balance out the oversized shirt. Like I said, Amber was very emaciated. Apparently she took the term "starving artist" literally. My many lavish dinners out with Charlie had definitely taken a toll on my hips, but he always told me that I was more beautiful than any woman he had ever seen.

Again, I had to stop myself from thinking about Charlie. Charlie and his compliments, Charlie and his rugged good looks, Charlie and his intoxicating eyes...

Jackson interrupted my indulgent thoughts yet again with his booming voice. "Are you about ready? That is the only bathroom in the place and I would really like to brush my teeth before we go out."

"Oh, I'm sorry. You can come in. I'm dressed now."

"Damn." He grinned at me. "Well, I guess I really should brush my teeth then."

We left his loft without cleaning anything up. Even the tray of fruit and baked goods was still on the bed where we left it just a few moments ago.

This would have never happened at Charlie's. He was such a neat freak. There couldn't be a dish in the sink when we left or it would ruin his whole night.

Jackson seemed to take life so casually, like he would get to things when he wanted to. I mean, what other guy would just decide to make a chocolate cake from scratch on a lonely Friday night? He really did go where the wind blew him.

Speaking of wind.

As soon as we stepped out onto the stairs, a gush of wind crashed against us and sent shivers down my entire body. At that moment, I was incredibly grateful for the sweatshirt and the fact that I was not wearing my little black dress from the night before.

Jackson, dressed in jeans, a long sleeved t-shirt and a beanie cap, took the scarf that was twirled around him and placed it around my neck. "So, Emmie, what would you say to a little shopping?"

I really wasn't expecting him to say that. I had my fill of shopping when I was with Charlie. Before, there was nothing I wanted or needed to shop for. I suddenly looked down at my ill-fitting, borrowed attire. Wait, scratch that, I had nothing to my name right now.

"Well, maybe that isn't a bad idea."

Jackson took me through the most amazing part of town with shops on every corner. These weren't the snooty kind of stores I had come across before with designer labels on every identical fabric. We went to consignment shops and vintage stores where no two garments were the same.

I was reminded of my first trip when I found my beloved green dress. I floated through the aisles of used clothing and ran my fingers down the wools and linens and cottons.

Jackson didn't hover over me like Charlie would. He seemed to be just as interested in the store's many fascinating elements as I was. However, the clothes were not what seemed to be piquing his curiosity. He was lingering over a box of old records, eyes wide as a child on Christmas morning fingering through the vinyl discs in wonderment. What a fascinating creature he was. I had never encountered someone like him before; definitely not in New York anyway.

"Wow! That is a great necklace. Did you get that around the corner at Crystal's place?" The young girl behind the counter who couldn't have been a day over seventeen beamed at me and reached her hand out to touch the baubles circling my neck.

"Oh, no, do you mean this? This is just something I put together a while ago." My face flushed crimson as the girl kept admiring my necklace while only keeping about three inches between us. Apparently she had never heard of the term personal space before.

"You did this? No, I don't believe it. This is great! But I've never seen your shop. Are you a local?"

I took a step back and her hand lost the grasp on my necklace. "No. I mean, yes I am local but I don't have a shop." *I used to sell stuff from home, but no one on Fifth Avenue wanted anything to do with my jewelry.*

"Well, you should. I mean, I see a hundred girls coming in and out of here looking for stuff like this, and I usually just send 'em down to Crystal, but I have never seen anything like that."

She popped her gum and went back to folding the stack of sweaters that she was working on before she grabbed me.

"No, I've never seen anything like her either." Jackson smirked as he walked past me and the close talking salesgirl.

Again, my cheeks were as bright red as Rudolph's nose.

"So Emmie, have you found anything you might want to wear. I mean, that is, unless you just want to live in my old sweats for a while."

The thought was actually rather pleasant. I could get used to his smell all over me. It was so intoxicating.

"This looks about your size, and it would go great with your necklace." Again, teasing me, he held up a rust colored pea coat that was absolutely amazing.

"Wow, where did you get this? It's great!" I looked at the wool fabric and intricate stitching and detailing. In an uptown store, this coat would have gone for a thousand dollars. A stifling thought suddenly hit me. I had absolutely no money. Well, that wasn't exactly true. I had that emergency twenty dollar bill, but how would I live on that?

Once again my face must have given away what was trudging around in my brain because Jackson said, "Well, you are just going to have to let me pay for this because I need to repay you for keeping up my reputation as a swinging bachelor." He snatched the red coat out of my hands and marched to the counter with it.

"What?" He took me completely off-guard with that comment.

"All of my neighbors saw you sneaking into my apartment last night. You are helping to maintain my womanizer status. Every great artist must know how to maltreat women or they just can't think about becoming famous."

"I doubt you have any idea on how to mistreat a lady." I was only half joking of course. He knew how to push my buttons, that was for sure, but he treated me with the utmost respect when it counted. "Well, I really couldn't let you pay for that Jack. It just wouldn't be proper."

"Proper? Really? You sure are an old soul Em. And by the way, I have never wanted to be anything close to proper in my life. I've got this. Why don't you go model some skirts for me, show me what I am missing underneath that jumble of sweats. There are some really short ones over on that rack against the wall, perfect for a cold New York winter." He chuckled to himself as he threw the amazing coat on top of his stack of records and pulled out a large wad of green bills from his back pocket.

He always seemed to have cash. I was so used to Charlie paying for everything on credit that it had been quite a long time since I had seen anyone pay for anything with cash. It was almost taboo in Charlie's world, like you weren't *somebody* until you had a gold card.

"Gina, you have got to see this necklace. The girl says she made it, but I think she is just yankin' my chain."

The shop girl was sitting on the counter with her legs piled up against her, twirling the phone cord around her finger and whispering to whoever was on the other end of the line. It was also kind of interesting to me that her phone even still had a cord, but it looked just as antique as everything else around here.

"Looks just like one of Crystal's, but from the looks of her, she couldn't have afforded Crystal's stuff." I opened my mouth to argue with her, but she quickly continued. "Yeah, come down now and look. Alright, bye."

She popped the gum she was chewing and hopped down from the counter. She stared at me as she hung up the ancient phone and walked over to where Jackson was standing.

"You all set?" She popped her gum again, looking painfully impatient, as if he had taken her away from something way more important than doing her job.

"Uh, I'm not sure. Emmie, was there anything else here that caught your eye?" They both glared at me, waiting for my reply.

"No, no, you get your stuff. I'm fine."

"Ok then, guess no use beatin' a dead horse. You will have to live in this coat. Although," a menacing grin spread across his unshaved face, "that could be an interesting prospect." His eyes rolled into his head as he envisioned God knows what.

Suddenly, a loud thumping noise came from the behind the counter and a woman with ultra violet highlights strewn through her blonde hair emerged from the darkened staircase.

She was about the same height as I was, but looked as if she hadn't eaten a thing in ten years. She could have probably been mistaken for a man, lacking any curves at all, but her face was devastatingly beautiful and unmistakably womanly.

"What was worth dragging me away from my favorite soap Laura? Desmond was just about to tell Katarina about his twin brother Felix." She groaned at the young cashier, her arms folded around her chest like she was giving herself a hug.

The girl said nothing, but nodded her head in my direction while I stood there pretending I was looking at the rack of scarves. The woman who had descended from the back staircase sighed and dragged her feet over to where I was. My face began to flush. I wasn't exactly sure what was happening. Was she checking me out?

She stopped at the end of the rack and took in a long meaningful breath before speaking a word to me. She was staring at my necklace and although I was completely uncomfortable, I was also happy that someone had taken notice to my quality craftsmanship. The "uptown" girls wanted nothing to do with my jewelry because there weren't diamonds or rubies in them.

"Huh," was all she said.

She twirled like a ballerina in Converse sneakers, around the rack to get a better view of my necklace. In any other situation, I would have tried to hide or run away, but being in this place, and being with Jackson brought out a courageous side of me that I hadn't felt since before Charlie.

I reached around to unclasp the string of beads from my neck. Before she got around to me, I had it dangling from my fingertips and held it in her face.

"Here, you can get a closer look this way."

"Oh! Uh, thanks." She grabbed it from my hands and poured the stringed beads into her palm like a stream of water. Examining every millimeter of the trinket, her face looked slightly less impressed as the girl behind the counter. Watching her look at it like that, with questioning eyes, I began to get self-conscious and felt the need to defend my life's passion.

"I know it isn't fancy, but I'm more of a simple girl myself and that is what I like. I didn't make it for anyone else. It was really one of my first pieces, when I was just learning how to do it, so if you are looking at the beadwork I know it's not great." I reached out to snatch it back from her so that she couldn't tell me how awful it really was. I was already mortified and she hadn't even spoken a word about it.

"Relax, uh, what is your name?"

"Emmie." I was still standing in front of her with my palm stretched out.

"Relax *Emmie*. It's good. No, I shouldn't say that, it's damn good." She put her empty hand on my outstretched arm and forced it down to my side. "Laura, you said she didn't get this from Crystal's place, right?"

"Listen, I don't know what you are talking about, but.." I was really starting to get embarrassed, them talking about me as if I wasn't standing right in front of them.

"Emmie, sweetie," she interrupted me. "Do you have more stuff like this?" She held up my necklace in her palm, unwilling to let me have it back. Her eyebrow arched upward while she awaited my reply.

"Um, yeah, I've got a bunch of boxes at Char, uh, at my old place. Why?"

A huge grin ran across her magnificent face, "My dear, how would you like to work out a deal with me?"

She threw her arm around my shoulder and led me through a beaded curtain into the back of the tiny shop. Jackson shot me a dashing smile himself and went back to sifting through the racks.

He seemed to trust these girls, but I wasn't sure if I should be scared, intrigued, or just happy that someone was showing an interest in my jewelry. Either way, I let her talk.

Chapter 6...

"So, do we have a deal or what?" she waited for me to speak now, even though I wasn't able to get a word in edge-wise for the past ten or fifteen minutes.

"Yes, yes we do." I was almost jumping out of my seat from excitement. I tried to keep it together and not look as young as I actually was. It was a good trick I had learned from my years with Charlie. Most of his clients and business partners were much older than me and I didn't want to look like a child to them, so I learned how to behave how I assumed a mature woman would in most circumstances. It was increasingly hard to do that right now though when I was holding back the urge of screaming, "yahoo!" right into her face.

"Well, you just get me some more of your jewelry from...where did you say it was?" she asked.

Crap. I stared at her like a deer in headlights and said absolutely nothing.

"Well, anyway, just get it and get back here. And don't worry about that coat. It's on me." She said as she pushed me back through the curtain and out to where Jackson was patiently waiting for me.

"Thank you! Thanks so much." I turned back to share my gratitude but she had already disappeared back up the stairs. I guess she didn't forget about her soap opera.

"So, what was that all about?" Jackson smiled, holding two large bags in his hands and heading towards the door.

"Wait! She said I could have that coat!" I cried out to him. I really wanted that coat, and this way it wasn't charity. I will earn it!

"Oh come on Emmie. It's already in the bag. Let's get out of here so you can tell me about the fifteen minute conversation that I was unable to eavesdrop on from behind these thick walls." He opened the door for me and we walked out of the shop before I opened my mouth again.

As soon as we were out in the cold air, he grabbed the coat from one of his bags and draped it around my shoulders. I quickly put my arms through the sleeves and it fit perfectly. I knew it would. Unconsciously, I twirled around like a little girl in a new party dress.

"Perfect."

"It is, isn't it?" I was beaming in this second hand coat. I kept twirling, not caring that I was out in public for everyone to see.

"Yes, just perfect." He reiterated, smiling again. "Ok, so what was that all about?"

"Oh, Jackson, you will never believe it! Gina, I guess you wouldn't know her name was Gina, well that was the woman who took me back into her office. At least I think it was her office. I am not really sure. Well, anyway, Gina told me that she loved my jewelry and that they've been looking for a way to compete with this Crystal lady down the street.

She used to have her stuff here but then they had this falling out of sorts and she went down the street and took half of their customers with her. Apparently her stuff isn't as good as mine, or so Gina says, and she thinks that if I could come and sell my jewelry here that she would be able to get more people in here and in essence "stick it" to Crystal for jumping ship like that. So, she wanted to know if I would bring some of it here to show her and see how things go. Can you believe it?" I somehow got all of that out in one breath. I inhaled quickly and looked at him with the biggest smile on my face, waiting for his response.

Jackson just started laughing. I could tell he meant no harm in it, so I didn't get offended. I probably looked a little crazy with excitement, so I started laughing too.

"Well, I always had faith in you." He joked.

"You didn't even know I made jewelry!" I hit him on the shoulder.

"So, I guess this means you are going to have to go back home sooner than you thought?" his voice turned a little more serious and he looked at me with a concerned stare.

Dammit! I was so excited about this new venture that I kept forgetting about having to go get my stuff at Charlie's. I was sort of hoping that after a few years had passed, maybe a decade or two, he would just decide to send me my things and I would never have to deal with the fact that I left him standing there in that restaurant with a ring in his hand. But like my momma always told me, you can't pay the rent on hopes and dreams.

"Yeah, I guess I do." My excitement ceased at the prospect of having to face Charlie again.

"Well, let's get you out of my clothes and into some of your new threads, shall we?" he grabbed my hand with his and hailed a cab for us back to his apartment. Apparently he had a few secrets of his own while I was talking with Gina. Those bags weren't full of records, they were full of clothes, and I had an inkling that he hadn't taken himself on a shopping spree today.

"I still can't believe you did this Jackson. You really shouldn't have bought me all of these things. I have to pay you back. I promise you I will get you this money back as soon as I sell some of my jewelry." I was talking to him through his   bedroom door that had recently become my own while he politely took the couch like a gentleman.

"When you are rich and famous, just remember the little people." He snickered. "Are you almost ready?"

After our big outing at the thrift shop last week, Jackson had taken a few days off of to spend some time getting me acclimated to my new surroundings, since I would be calling this place home from now on.

He had managed to show me around the whole neighborhood, giving me lessons on fine New York cuisine which included the best pizza shop and the most amazing candy store imaginable tucked inside a warehouse, and gave me an in-depth tutorial of the arts and music that made this place come alive. Where New York City thrived in business, this place found its niche in the more cultural aspects of life. It was the blood sweat and tears of the people.

He bought me a few more outfits here and there while we were out on the town until I almost had a full wardrobe of new clothes. It had been like a mini vacation spending every day with him, but I was starting to feel like he was my benefactor or something.

I would definitely have to find a way to pay him back sometime soon. I mean, he wasn't like Charlie, running a fortune 500 company, and here I was letting him pay my way through society. But he seemed to enjoy every moment we spent together and never mentioned money at all.

Being a realtor, especially in this extremely tough real estate market, he had plenty of time to pal around town with me, but I felt like he had been putting a few things off on my account.

Some part of me was secretly happy about that though; that he was willing to put aside other things to spend time with me. That was the problem me and Charlie had all along, and that was what our downfall was inevitably. And that was the reason I was getting ready to go face the music and get that issue resolved to be able to move on with my new life, minus Charlie.

I took another look at myself in his miniscule mirror. Was I ready for this? Probably not, but it had to happen, right? I straightened out the wrinkled cardigan I had thrown over a small white tank top and a boot cut pair of jeans Jackson had picked out for me.

How he knew my size was beyond me, and frankly, something I didn't want to think about. It was one of the most comfortable outfits I had ever worn, short of my flannel pajamas, and it was a good thing. I would need to be as comfortable as possible to do this.

"Emmie? Emmmmmie, Emmie, Emmie Bo Bemmie, bananafana fo femmie, me mi mo memmie, Emmie!" I opened the door just in time to catch him drumming the side of the couch with his fingers, apparently amusing his self in song.

"Ok, I think I'm ready." I groaned, inhaling in hopes to find some strength in the air.

"The clothes look great, if I do say so myself." He was never a humble man.

"Yes, you *are* good at picking out women's clothing. Perhaps you should look into that as a career prospect. You know, if the whole silly real estate thing doesn't pan out." I laughed. It was so easy to joke with him because he rarely got offended.

"Well, the way the market is looking, I just may have to give Bloomingdale's a call." He hopped over the back of the couch, reached out his arm and said, "Shall we?"

"Oh…Jack," I wasn't quite sure how to say this the right way. "I was thinking that maybe I should go alone. I mean, it has only been a week you know? I can't exactly show up on his doorstep after a week with some strange guy to get my stuff. What would he think of me?"

He dropped his arm and took a step back from me. Apparently he wasn't as indestructible as I thought. He looked as if I had just smacked him in the face.

"No, I don't mean it like that. You're not a *stranger*, well, not to me anyway. I just mean I don't want to hurt his feelings, you know?" I could see I had already hurt Jackson's though.

"Yeah, that's fine." His tone changed into something I had never heard before.

"Jack, I…"

"No, I said its fine. Anyway, I've got a lot to do today. It'll be nice to have the house to myself for the afternoon so I can work on some stuff. I've been putting a lot off since you got here." He flung himself back on the couch, like a hurt puppy dog.

I didn't really know what to say or what to do, so I stood there for a couple moments and just stared at the sneakers he had painstakingly picked out for me. They caught his eye because they were stark white and he had a crazy notion to paint green and pink checkers all over them so that I would stand out in a crowd if he ever lost me. It was a strange, but rather sweet gesture.

Looking at those shoes, I realize that he was not just some "strange man," he was my friend and I had hurt his feelings. After everything he had done for me, after being there for me when I needed him most, I had hurt him too. I could almost cry standing there. But I didn't want to cry, I wanted to make him feel better.

I sat down next to him on the couch and grabbed his hand. "Jack, you know I really appreciate everything that you have done for me, I really, really do. I don't know where I'd be without you."

Homeless, that's where I'd be.

"It has nothing to do with you, I just think it would be best if I went there alone, for Charlie's sake, you know."

He released his hand from mine and smugly said, "Yeah, sure. For *Charlie*. Do whatever you gotta do. I told you, I've got plans." Then he picked up his guitar and ignored me while plucking at the strings.

I could see there was no getting out of this debacle now. I would try and repair the mess I had made here with Jackson just as soon as I finish going through the hell I was going to face with Charlie. I took what was left of my shattered pride and stood up.

"We are still on for takeout right?" I didn't know what else to say, but I had to know that I hadn't just destroyed things here in my only safe haven.

"Yeah, sure Emmie, take out." He was still strumming his guitar and pretending I was already gone. I took that as my cue.

Great, this would not make this afternoon any easier.

Chapter 7...

For some reason the cab was extra cold and I huddled deep in the linings of my new green coat-the coat that Jackson had purchased for me on our first day out and snuck in the bag before I had a chance to tell him not to spend money on me.

That kind of reminded me of Charlie, but Charlie would have flaunted the purchase and made me show it off to everyone we saw. He also would have never let me buy anything second hand like that. It just wasn't done when you had enough pocket change to buy small foreign countries. But I was so thankful for this coat, and for Jackson, and I couldn't help thinking about how I had hurt him today.

But why? Why was he hurt? I mean, we were just friends.

We were *friends*, right?

The past week had been so great spending time with him and yes there might have been some casual flirting here and there, but I assumed we were just friends. He was really the only friend I had right now. I had to stop thinking about this and get my head in the game.

The cab pulled up in front of Charlie's building sooner than I was ready for and I felt my stomach doing back flips. If I had enough strength to actually get out of the cab and walk into the building, who knows if I would be able to drag myself into the elevator, endure the ride up to his floor, and then once I was there, would I be able to actually KNOCK?

I could see this process was going to take a lot more than I had anticipated, but if I wanted my jewelry, and my life back, I would have to muster up all of my cowardly lion courage and put two feet in front of the other.

Tell that to my feet.

I slinked out of the cab, after giving him the money Jackson had lent me. I really had to start paying him back. I reminded myself that was why I was here. To get my jewelry and get a job so that I could pay Jackson back for all of the kindness he has bestowed upon me. That would get me to the elevator at least, right?

Harry, the older gentleman who was the doorman to the building recognized me at once and tipped his hat at me. He didn't smile or greet me as he had done for the past year that I had known him. In fact his face was turned down and looked as if he was upset about something.

I immediately became self-conscious, thinking he must know what happened. I can't imagine that Charlie would have spilled the beans though. He was the most private person I have ever known when it came to personal matters. He was all business outside of his home. So I wonder how Harry would have found out.

I smiled at him and said, "Hey Harry. How's the weather today?"

The weather was always something safe to discuss.

"Looks like it might rain ma'am." He still didn't smile, but he tipped his hat back onto his head and gave me a pat on the shoulder as I walked past him into the building. It was actually a pretty sunny day so I gave him a confused look. Then it hit me.

He definitely knew.

The pit in my stomach grew to the size of a grapefruit. I knew how much Charlie hated people knowing his business. I also knew that he hated people feeling sorry for him. I was becoming a regular man-destroyer these days, wasn't I? Kick 'em when they're up, kick 'em when they're down.

Walking through the lobby, I saw familiar faces all around me. Faces that used to greet me every day with a smile. Faces that were now doing their best to look in any direction other than my own. My courage was dwindling rapidly. How was I ever going to do this? If the random people in this lobby could intimidate me this much, how could I face Charlie?

I tucked my head down and walked as fast as I could to the elevator. The eyes were still on me, although no one was looking at me. It wasn't until the steel doors shut that I felt safe. But I knew that was only for a matter of moments.

My finger instinctively reached out to push the "down" button. I was reverting to animal instincts now and smelling danger usually warrants a swift retreat. I pulled it back though and jammed it into my pocket. Not because I was ready for this; mostly I was too cowardice to walk through the lobby again.

I pushed the P button (remembering the first time Charlie took me to his home and how I never knew there were actual people, not just movie stars, who lived in Manhattan penthouse apartments) and swallowed the panic that was clawing its way up from my chest.

I fought back my overwhelming urge to pull the emergency lever. That would only make me more of a spectacle anyway. There was no turning back now. I couldn't go back now. I had to face this. I was really regretting telling Jackson I would go at this alone. Who was I kidding? I can't do this alone? I needed moral support. Lots and lots of moral support.

The elevator ride was shorter than I had ever remembered it being. When it made its final beep and thudded to a halt at the penthouse floor, I heard the doors beginning to open.

Here goes nothing.

This was weird. I didn't know what to do. Was I supposed to knock? Should I use my key? He couldn't have changed it in a week's time, could he? Would he? It wasn't exactly like I would have trusted me right now. I ripped his heart out before we even got dessert. I would've changed the locks.

Knocking sounded like a good idea.

I lifted up my trembling arm to the door and gave it a few swift raps. I didn't want to seem pushy, but I also didn't know if I could knock again if he didn't hear me. Maybe he wouldn't be home and I could do this sight unseen. No worries in that.

I could hear a scuffle inside and took a few steps back from the door when I saw the knob turning. I felt like I might vomit.

When the door swung open, I was stunned. There before me stood a man, early thirties with brown hair and matching eyes with what seemed to be the start of a beard. He was dressed in gray jogging pants and an oversized t-shirt and he looked as if he had just climbed out of bed. He was unkempt and quite a mess of a man, but underneath all of the mess, I saw a familiar face.

"Charlie?" I didn't really have to ask, I would have known him anywhere, but I just couldn't believe my eyes.

"Em!" he was startled to see me, I could tell, but this wasn't the miserable surprise I was expecting. "Uh hey, hi, hi." He struggled to smooth out his rumpled clothing and haggard appearance. It wasn't working. I had never seen him like this.

"Um, I'm sorry to just drop by unannounced…"

"Oh no, no, don't be silly, come in come in. I'm, uh, just.." he looked around the room as if he was trying to explain away his situation. He seemed to come up with nothing. "You know, work got busy and so I was taking a break for a little while and I gave the cleaning lady the day off." Trying to smile, I could see how flustered he really was. "Come in, come in."

I walked past him, taking stock of this sullied apartment that I had never once seen with a speck of dust lingering around, while he hurried to pick up dirty clothes and dishes along our way to the living room.

"I could come back at another time if you are busy."
I knew that was a lie before it even came out of my mouth. I
could never do this again. I just wasn't strong enough.

"No, no, it's fine. I was just getting some things
together for a deposition I have on Thursday. Have a seat."
He pointed to the couch that was covered in random papers
and a blanket. Quickly he scurried ahead of me to clear a
place for me to sit. I was so thrown aback by the whole
situation that I forgot to be nervous about why I was there.

I wiggled my way between two mounds of clothes
on the couch and sat down. I was still not sure what to say,
or how to say it, but luckily the mess of a room kept my
attention long enough for me to get casual words out.

"So, how have you been?" Wait. That was probably
the wrong thing to say. Did I want to hear either answer? If
he had been good, that would mean I meant very little to
him, and if he hadn't been good, that would mean that I had
crushed him. I quickly tried to retract my statement.

"How's work been? Busy I guess, huh?" I asked,
arching my question around the cluttered room.

"Uh, yeah, busy. I've got a few things I'm working
on right now."

He looked so frazzled. I had never seen him like this since I had known him. He was always put together. Calm, cool and collected, that was Charlie. This man was just out of sorts.

"So, uh, where have you been staying?" He asked and then I suppose he wanted to retract his question to by the look on his face.

Also not a question I particularly knew how to answer.

"Well, I have been staying here and there with friends, you know." I tried to dodge the bullet and get as far away from having to explain Jackson as possible. "But I just got some really great news, which is actually the reason I am here today."

His face shifted down to his knees, as if he was expecting me to say that seeing him was the reason I was there today. He did his best to perk himself up immediately so I wouldn't see but I had already caught him.

"You know my jewelry? Well I was wearing this one piece I had made, nothing fancy or anything and this shop owner down in So Ho told me she loved it and wants me to come showcase it in her store. Isn't that just crazy?"

My own inner excited emotions were brimming to the surface as I told him my news. I wanted to tone it down and not act so happy that good things were happening for me while he was looking so miserable, but I could barely control myself.

"You were in So Ho?" His mellow voice seemed somewhat concerned. I forgot how he felt about me being in such unknown parts of town for him.

I reverted back to his naïve girlfriend who had to hide the adventurous side of myself from him. "Well no, I mean, I was just walking and saw this shop."

"Em, you really need to be careful in those…" He stopped himself. "Well, anyway, I was wondering where you went that night. You could've come home, you know."

Both of us sat there awkwardly, not knowing what to say. I couldn't tell him I ran to another man just moments after I rejected his marriage proposal. Thankfully, he broke the silence.

"So I guess that brings you to why you are here now? I mean, you are here to get your stuff?" Again, I saw the sad puppy. Did he think that I had changed my mind and was coming home? That gut-wrenching pit was growing inside of me again. Had I just got his hopes up and was now crushing him, again?

"Well, no Charlie, I mean, I am sorry I left everything here for you to have to deal with. I really should have moved my mess out of your way. I just…"

He hopped off the couch with a new determination. "Oh, ok. I haven't moved anything of yours. I mean, I don't know what you need but you don't have to take everything right now." He stopped as he thought about what he had just said. "Well, I just mean that you can keep some stuff here if you don't have a permanent place yet."

He was trying so hard to be his normal self that it was awkward for the both of us. Why couldn't we just talk about the elephant in the room and act like normal people? Why all of these games and hidden emotions? I decided to be the person I imagined I was and speak up.

"Charlie, I know this is hard."

He looked at me with the eyes I had known for years; eyes that I had fallen deep into so many times before; eyes that I hadn't seen since that cold snowy night when we said goodbye to each other. He interrupted me before I could get too deep into my conversation

"Em, do you think we could have coffee sometime soon?" He tried his best to smile, but his eyes were showing a very vulnerable side that I had never really seen in Charlie. "I mean, it just feels like the way we left everything was so unfinished. And you know me, I have to finish my business or it weighs on me."

I did know that. He never left the office until everything on his desk was in its place. That's usually why I went to bed alone. And that's why seeing this place like this was so unnerving.

"I would really like that Charlie." I smiled back at him, my own vulnerability showing. I was starting to fall down a slippery slope right into his eyes, so I pulled back the reigns and remembered why I was there.

"Well I know you are probably busy so I won't keep you. I just have to grab a few boxes of my jewelry."

I got up and being the gentleman that he was he stood up with me.

"Yes, I should really get back to.." he looked around the mess of a room we were now standing in, "well, I had better call the cleaning lady and have her take care of some of this mess."

He gathered up a couple of shirts that were strewn across the coffee table and put them in a pile on the chair. How that was any better, I didn't know, but it seemed to appease him.

"So, Em...coffee?"

"Absolutely Charlie, what about next Wednesday?" I knew that Wednesdays were usually a good day because his schedule was lighter in the afternoons due to the board meetings the company had in the morning. It hadn't been long enough for me to forget his schedule. It hadn't been long enough for me to forget anything. It had only been a week. Was that right? A week?

"Um, yeah. Wednesday is just fine. Let's say one o clock?" He was still doing his best to clean up around me, as well as avoiding looking me in the eyes.

"I can meet you at Mink's around the corner from your office, is that ok? Or maybe you have a better idea, I mean, it's just a suggestion." For some reason I wanted his approval. I had not yet regained my strong woman status where I could stand behind my decisions; even a decision about where to meet for coffee. He had a way of making me feel like I needed him to tell me what to do.

"Mink's is fine. The coffee there is always really good."

He always seemed to forget that I hated coffee. But I would suck it up, for Charlie. And deep down, I felt like things were unfinished between us as well. Funny, because last week I thought we had wrapped everything up neatly and tied it with a bright bow.

I grabbed a few boxes that I knew I had put my jewelry in and hobbled around until I got them straight in my arms.

"Here let me get those for you." Charlie said, reaching out his arms to steady me.

"No, no, I'm fine. I got 'em, really." I honestly wasn't sure I had them at all, but I couldn't bear to have him help me carry those boxes down to the street and have an awkward goodbye there in front of the doorman and all of his nosey neighbors.

"Well at least let me get the door for you. I swear woman, you are so stubborn when it comes to a man helping you." He smiled, and this time it was lighthearted and looked completely sincere.

"Although I may not have always encouraged it, don't think I didn't appreciate everything you have done for me Charlie." I smiled back and I could feel my emotions about to crash over me. Now would be a good time to exit.

"Huhmm!" He cleared his throat. "Well Wednesday it is then and I will keep good care of the rest of your boxes." He looked like my last statement was about to affect him too so I made a speedy departure out the door with my two large packages in hand.

"Bye Charlie." I said facing the elevator and not daring to look back as I pushed the button. Tears were welling and any sudden movement would surely cause them to fall down my cheeks.

"See ya Em."

I heard the door close behind me.

What had I just witnessed in there? What were we doing? Who was that emotionally muddled man I had just spent the last twenty minutes with?

This was not what I would have assumed would happen. Not that I wanted him to move on after a week or anything, but I didn't know that his life would just stop in place.

I guess somewhere deep down inside, there was that very human part of me that was just slightly pleased that I meant that much to him. I mean, I'm not going to lie; I am glad that I didn't see him smiling and acting cheerful.

But this, this shell of a man; this made me feel that tinge of guilt as if I were the sole entity that had destroyed him. And being with him today, seeing him without the job and the millions of   other distractions that tore us apart gave me a strange uneasiness and left me pining for the life that we had before.

I rode the elevator down to the lobby pondering what I had just seen. My big strong man, my savior on the park streets, was now just a crumpled shell. What had I done to him? And why was I starting to feel like I had made a huge mistake?

Chapter 8...

The sound of fingers delicately plucking a guitar welcomed me into the apartment that I had called home for the last few days. I was worried what kind of a mess I would come back to, being as when I left Jackson was not all that thrilled with me. To find him playing guitar was a relief. He always seemed in a good mood when he played.

I slid the boxes I was carrying on the counter by the door and quietly closed it behind me while I tiptoed into the kitchen. I felt like I was literally walking on eggshells so as not to disturb him. I wasn't quite sure how to start this conversation either. Why do I keep putting myself in these situations with men? Was I destined to hurt every man I came into contact with?

Scanning the apartment, I saw him.

Jackson was sitting Indian style in a pair of faded blue jeans and a tight white tank top that showed off his manly physique. For a realtor, he was surprisingly strapping. His taught muscles flexed with each movement of his fingers across the bridge of his guitar.

The ripples flowed across his back melodically with the rhythm of the song he was playing. He hadn't heard me come in the door so I crouched down onto the floor by the kitchen counter and enjoyed the view.

He was staring out the large warehouse window at the edge of the apartment that looked out over the whole neighborhood. I couldn't see clearly, but even with his picturesque city view, I was sure his eyes were closed. Whenever I saw him sing and play he closed his eyes.

So far, he was just plucking around with a melody but I watched him tilt his head and start humming to himself. The humming shortly turned into words.

Unfortunately, he was singing so quietly that I couldn't make out any of the lyrics.

I really wanted to hear what he was singing. I imagined the most beautiful lyrics; speaking of a beautiful and magical love. Again, I secretly hoped he was singing about me. However, strangely enough, this time it also made me think of Charlie.

I wanted to hear the words he was mumbling so badly that I tried to stretch my body closer into the living room. I should have known better than to trust my own feet.

As I leaned in, my ankles gave way under my body and I found myself in a dangerous predicament; flailing towards the ground. Trying desperately to stop myself, my arms instinctively reached up to grab something to break my fall.

Regrettably, the only thing I came up with was a huge pile of pots that had been put there to be washed. They not only failed in stopping me from falling over, they fell on top of me, along with everything inside of them. They also made the loudest crashing sound as they fell all over the kitchen.

Without looking, I knew my cover had been completely blown. I just laid there, eyes closed and surrounded by the calamity I had created on the floor.

Seeing as the whole building probably heard me, it was obvious that Jackson did as well.

When I finally mustered up the courage to peek through one eye, I could see his glistening chiseled body standing over me. He was holding back his giggles but I noticed a small twinge of worry on his face as well. Good! For all he knew I could have a concussion or head trauma; not exactly something to chuckle about!

His guitar had been tossed aside somewhere between my crashing and this very embarrassing moment as he was standing over me with his arms folded across his chest. He kept his eyebrow raised as he attempted to keep a stern face, like I was a child who had been caught red handed in the cookie jar. I must have looked really pathetic though because I could see the smile creeping up on his lips.

I reached up to push the metal lid that had fallen on top of my chest to the ground and with that he lost all composure. He burst into beads of laughter while I proceeded to pick soggy noodles out of my hair. Luckily it was the pasta pot that fell and not the one that he had cooked his tomato sauce in last night or my face would have been red, literally.

"What on Earth are you doing to my kitchen Emmie?" He managed to get out through his fits of laughter.

He reached down and pulled a noodle off of my shoulder and flung it at the wall. Charlie would have thrown a fit if I had made such a mess in the kitchen. This didn't seem to do anything but humor Jackson as he grabbed me under the arm and helped me to my careless feet.

"I was, uh, I was just coming into the living room and I must have tripped on something." Sounded like a viable story, right?

"Oh, I see." He sounded very skeptical as he crouched down to help me pick up the pots and put them in the sink. "I thought maybe you were sneaking up on me."

I couldn't see his face as it was turned down to the ground, but I could hear the smile emanating from his lips. He couldn't have known what I was doing, could he? Immediately my face turned into a tomato.

"You forget about reflections in windows?" he chuckled.

"You saw me? Then why didn't you...why didn't you stop playing?" I was immediately furious that he had witnessed my entire fiasco.

"I was enjoying you watching me." His smile was coyer this time, more seductive on his face. "I like that you like my music."

Now he was the one turning red. Was Jackson really embarrassed? He just never seemed the type to me. I always assumed he had no shame whatsoever.

"I thought you'd still be mad at me." Why on Earth do I bring stuff up when it might have been forgotten?

"Why? Because you wanted to go see your ex by yourself? Told ya, I had things I had to do too." And just like that, his attitude from this morning had returned.

He finished picking up all the pots and turned around towards the couch where he had a tiny piece of scrap paper laying on the cushion. "Speaking of getting things done," he handed me the note and walked back towards the window, "your friend from the clothing shop called and she said something about you getting a place there?"

I forgot she had told me that if I needed a place to stay, I could stay in the storage room above the shop until I got things situated. At the time, it sounded great, since I was still sponging off of Jackson. I never thought he would be mad about that, but it had been really nice living here with him for this past week.

"Well, yeah, I just figured you were probably sick of me making you sleep on the couch all these nights and would want your space again. You know, to be the quintessential bachelor that you always wanted to be." I was trying to make light of the situation, but it wasn't working as I had hoped.

"Yeah, sure." He said smugly. "Be nice to have my own space again."

Today was obviously going to be the day for smoothing things over, and I was the one who had to do it, so here goes. It seemed to work with Charlie.

"Jackson, I can't tell you how much I appreciate everything you have done for me for the past week. I would literally be homeless and wearing that little black dress on the streets if you hadn't helped me."

I put a big puppy dog grin on my face, hoping that he would melt like butter and forgive me, just like Charlie. At this moment though, the look on his face told me that he was in fact not Charlie, and would not be melting as I had hoped.

"You can cut the crap speech that is supposed to make me feel better Em. I'm not your boyfriend remember? You don't owe me anything."

Wow. That fact was beyond false. I owed him everything.

"Jack…"

"No, just save it. It's fine. I was here when you needed me and now that you don't, sayonara sucker." He raised his arm to his forehead and saluted the air.

Ok, so this was not going as well as it had with Charlie. Should've seen that coming, but I didn't really expect Jackson to be this upset, it wasn't like him. I had to try a different approach.

"Jackson, this whole thing has just gotten way out of control, ya' know?"

I waited for him to walk away or interrupt me, but something about my statement seemed to perk his interests, and he didn't stop me from continuing, so I did. He crossed his arms over his chest, waiting to see how I would finish that thought.

"I mean, I don't really even know what we are doing here, with this living arrangement and you buying me clothes and paying my way. That's just not really what I'm into and I know you never signed up to be anyone's sugar daddy."

He scoffed and attempted to say something, but I kept on going, knowing that I probably wouldn't get another chance to say these things after today.

"And who are we kidding here, you said it yourself, you are not my boyfriend so you shouldn't feel the need to take care of me. You should be out dating artsy women and living the single life to its fullest and not playing house with a mess like me. You really don't want to get mixed up with me where I am now, I don't even know what I want out of life or where I am going from here. Until I figure that out, no one should…"

I couldn't finish. Or didn't know how to finish. A lot of those words felt hurtful, even to me, and I was directing them to Jackson. Somewhere in my rant I believe I had implied that he was interested in me, and that was probably far from the truth. And was I saying that I was too good for him, or for Charlie? I swallowed a huge lump of regret about my words, but my feelings were already starting to get cloudy about these two men, and it was best to just say what needed to be said and move on, right?

After I stopped, there was an awful silence in the room, as if a giant whale had swallowed us up whole. I didn't look at him, although I knew he was staring daggers at me. I could feel his hot eyes burning through my skin, but I couldn't move, couldn't speak, couldn't do anything but wait for him to explode and tell me off, as I deserved to be told off for saying all of those things to him.

I found the courage to look at him after a few moments of silence and I found, to my surprise, that he didn't look upset at all. In fact, I could swear he was about to give me that crooked smile of his or laugh in my face. I guess I deserved that too. He obviously wanted to laugh in my face, thinking that he wanted anything to do with me. Who did I think I was?

"Well, being as you've got that all figured out, I suppose there is nothing I could possibly say to you right now, huh?" Jackson said, through a cocky smirk. "But just so you know, I happen to think that you are not as much of a mess as you think you are. And also, while you were out today, I got myself a date."

I didn't know why, but that statement felt like something cut me across my chest.

"Oh...well...ok." Three words were all my brain could come up with at that moment.

"I mean, you are still welcome to stay here, ya' know, but it sounds like you've got bigger and better plans out there, so maybe you're right. Maybe we have been playing house and now it's time for you to grow up."

Again, pain across my chest. Now I believe he was just trying to hurt me, and if I must say, it worked.

That was the end of our conversation. As Jackson threw his guitar over his shoulder and walked out the door, I retreated to the bedroom with the sticky note of the shop owner's phone number. I figured the best thing I could do right now was to talk to her and tell her I was ready to come aboard.

"You can move in right away, the place is vacant," She told me. "Just make sure you bring your jewelry."

She didn't seem as excited as I was, but I could tell she was at least happy to talk to me. That feeling was few and far between around here so I got off the phone feeling like things were going to be ok.

Jackson didn't come home that night from his date until after I had gone to bed. I heard him stumbling around the kitchen for a few minutes and I laid there wondering if I should go talk to him.

I couldn't help but feel slightly jealous about him going out with some other woman, although I managed to push those feelings down. I mean, I had no right to feel that way since I was the one who kept saying that Jackson and I were just friends. Just friends. And I should be able to talk to my friend about anything, right? So why was I so nervous?

By the time I plucked up the courage to come out of the bedroom, he had already shut off the lights and was passed out on the couch. I guess that was my sign that he was done talking for today. Perhaps in the morning we could sort everything out and I could tell him that I was going to be out of his hair. That should make him happy.

Jackson was gone when I woke up and I didn't see him all afternoon. When it came time for me to leave, not even being able to say goodbye felt as if it was ripping me apart. It wasn't like it was goodbye forever, just "I'm moving to another place so that we can maintain a level of friendship that isn't ruined by my constant damaging ways." He had to understand that right?

I shoved the clothes Jackson had bought me into the black bag I picked up at Charlie's, along with my jewelry to show the girls at the shop. I held a few pieces in my hand as I positioned them in with my belongings.

My whole plan was revolving around this jewelry and I didn't even know if they would like it. They had only seen the piece I was wearing the day I met them. Who knows if they wouldn't just laugh me right out of the shop when I came waltzing in there with these pieces?

I had to stop myself from all of these self-deprecating thoughts because this plan was all I had right now. I had to have faith that this was all going to work out. It had to, right?

Walking around the bedroom, it felt so strange. I had only been there a little over a week, but I had grown accustomed to this place. The beautiful simplicity of Jackson's style was so inviting. His ratty old couch, the vibrant painted walls, the clutter of pots and pans strewn around the kitchen-it was like being at home. And the smell of musk whenever I opened the closet doors was more intoxicating than I could describe. I was definitely going to miss that smell every morning.

I ran my hands along the wall of the bedroom as I had done the first night I was there, stopping on the girl in the middle. That night I imagined I was her, smiling and reveling in the exciting colorful life I was embarking on. It seemed like no matter what was bursting around her, she was able to smile. It comforted me every day.

But now, in the light of midday as I was packing to leave this place and actually start over again, alone, I felt like she was mocking me. Somehow the smile wasn't contentment anymore. She was laughing at me, telling me I couldn't do this. I would be a failure and I would never find the kind of happiness she had amongst her rainbow.

I shook my head out of the negativity. I almost stuck my tongue out at her, and then I realized she was just a painting, so I bit it back and threw my bag over my shoulder. I looked around Jackson's apartment once more, dropped the spare key he had given me on the countertop and shut the door behind me.

Now, it was just me.

Alone.

On my own and facing the great unknown.

Crap.

Chapter 9.....

Gina wasn't there when I got to the shop. In fact, no one was there. Luckily she had given me a key or I would have been stuck standing on the street corner with all of my earthly belongings. I let myself in and went up the stairs to the room that was going to be mine for a little while. It was eerily quiet and I began to feel alone all over again. I quickly put it out of my mind and dropped my bags on the single bed in the middle of the room.

The place wasn't much to write home about, just a bed, dresser and a window that overlooked the street in front of the shop. I flopped down on the bed, shut my eyes and tried not to think about how scared I was or how all of this could crumble around me at any moment. Funny how your life can change in an instant, and then change again, and then change again without ever bothering to ask you how you feel about it.

After a few long silent moments and a few deep breaths, I sat up, grabbed my bag and began loading up the little dresser with all of my clothes. I might as well make myself at home. Most of the drawers were kind of rickety and I had a little trouble opening them, but in no time I had everything tucked neatly inside and put my empty bag in the corner of the room. So, this was home now.

After everything that had transpired with Jackson, I wasn't really looking forward to my lunch with Charlie. I know we had left things in on polite terms, but I couldn't help remembering the look on his face that night at the restaurant when I walked out on him and his ring. I also couldn't quite wrap my head around how much of a mess he was when we last saw each other at his apartment. It couldn't have been all about me, could it?

Well, feelings aside, I wasn't about to stand him up, so I got myself showered and sprayed on a perfume that he always seemed to enjoy and found myself standing in front of the mirror that Gina had let me borrow from downstairs.

I had been living here for only a few days now, but I managed to make it feel like my own space. Since I didn't have much, both Gina and the other girls who worked in the shop would find something they thought I would appreciate and randomly leave it on my doorstep. It was nice to be living above a consignment shop; you wouldn't believe the treasures people traded in.

I didn't have to start showing off my work until the following week because Gina thought she would give me some time to settle in to my surroundings before throwing me to the wolves. My first impression of her was completely wrong. I thought she was rough around the edges and the two of us might butt heads working and living so closely. Instead, she was incredibly compassionate, almost motherly, when it came to me. It was almost as if she could tell that the past few weeks had been rough on my soul so she took me under her wing while my heart healed.

I took one final look at myself in the mirror and headed out the door. It was a twenty minute cab ride to the place I would be meeting Charlie. Thankfully Gina had fronted me some pocket money to survive off of or it would have been a long walk uptown.

When we pulled up alongside the curb in front of the restaurant, I saw Charlie already sitting in a booth waiting for me. He looked more like himself today, not as disheveled as he was at his apartment, but there was still something not right about him. I paid the taxi driver and walked in to meet him.

He stood up when he saw me, always a gentleman, and said hello.

"Hi Charlie, you look dashing today."

"Oh, no, no, I just had a meeting this morning. You know, partners, clients, they expect you to look on top of your game." He rubbed at the front of his jacket, straightening out his tie, even though it was perfectly straight.

"Well, then they have the right man for the job, you are always on top of your game." It felt weird giving him compliments. As if I was leading him on or something.

"So, have you already ordered something?" I asked, knowing there was no way he would have ordered before I got there. That wasn't polite.

"Oh, no. I sat down and the lady brought me this coffee. I know you don't like coffee or I would have made sure she brought you one too. I mean, maybe you like coffee now? I am not sure. Do you want some?"

He looked so nervous, and I probably did too. This was stranger than I had anticipated it would be.

"Nope, still not a coffee drinker. Although I might just sniff your cup, you know how I love the smell of those beans." I chuckled a little, trying to break the ice.

He smiled a little. It was a start.

"However, I am very hungry, so I hope you haven't eaten yet."

"No, no, I haven't. That meeting started four hours ago and there were no donut breaks or anything." He smiled. He and I both knew even if there had been donut breaks, he never would've eaten them. He was perhaps one of the healthiest eaters on the planet. If it was a plant, he ate it. If it was made in a plant, he didn't.

Just as I slid my chair in, this young girl with seven different hair colors and just as many piercings stopped at the edge of our table and asked, "What can I get for you ma'am?"

Ma'am? Well, that's a first!

"Um, yes, could I have a large sweet tea please?" I said. We didn't even have menus so I don't know how we were going to eat, and I was starving, but I was kind of afraid to ask her. Especially after that ma'am comment.

"Could we please have two menus and we will need just a few moments to look them over before we decide what we will be ordering. Thank you."

I forgot exactly how take charge Charlie could be, even in a setting where it wasn't exactly warranted. But I was so thankful for it right now.

After being taken aback by his straightforward tone, the waitress nodded her head and headed towards the counter to grab our menus and quickly bring them to our table. It almost looked like she did a small curtsy as she was leaving but that could've been my imagination, although it wouldn't have been unjustified.

"I don't seem to remember the wait staff being so colorful the last time I was in here." He quietly chuckled as he ran his fingers through his hair. To anyone else, it would've sounded like an intensely judgmental and offensive statement, but I knew what he meant, and also that he meant no disrespect. That just wasn't what he was used to in his high society circles.

"Don't you know that rainbows are the new black these days?" I winked at him and he smiled.

I was trying to make him feel more comfortable, but my statement brought Jackson spiraling back into my head. Rainbows.

Ugh, push it away! You are here with Charlie you stupid girl!

I mentally smacked myself and tried to change the subject.

"So, I moved into a small room above the shop that wants to sell my jewelry. I'm all alone up there mostly but the girls are so nice downstairs." I don't know why I felt the need to tell him I was all alone, maybe to ease my conscience about shacking up with another man right after we broke up?

"Is that the place in So Ho?" He did his best to mask his obviously worried tone, but I could always see right through him.

Without even knowing it, the waitress had slid my sweet tea down in front of me and scampered away without a sound. I almost knocked it over as I tried to answer him.

"Yes, but it's really not as scary as you think. I know it's no Fifth Avenue, but"...

"I would like to come see some time. You know, I never got to see your art being displayed." He looked at me with those eyes. Those eyes that had always found a way into my soul when we were together. I quickly reached for my tea and took a long sip before I could get sucked in and lost forever.

"That's funny. You never called it "art" before. It was always just my hobby." It was the kind of thing that I would've wanted to say before but always kept to myself because I didn't want to upset him. But it was the truth, he never really thought what I did was anything worthwhile to the world. Not like his world of acquisitions and mergers and buying and selling stocks.

I could tell it took him by surprise, me saying something like that, and it looked as though he was going to say something, but instead he just frowned. I didn't know what to do, I almost apologized and grabbed his hand, but I knew neither of those things would be appropriate. Luckily he didn't stay silent for long.

"Emmie, part of the reason I wanted to meet with you was to apologize." He said in such a quiet voice that I almost had to lean in to hear him. I also didn't believe what I was hearing from him. *He* wanted to apologize to *me?* Shouldn't it be the other way around?

"I keep going over and over in my head where we went wrong in our relationship and I just keep seeing how I took you for granted. I just assumed you would be there. That you would always be the happy little woman sitting at home waiting for me to come home. I never even took into account that you had dreams of your own that you put on hold for me and my career."

"Char.." I tried to say and held my hand up to stop him…

"No, please, let me finish. I need to say this." He grabbed my hand in his and I felt a shiver go down my spine like the first time we met. "I know that you gave up so much for me, and I never gave back to you what you deserved. It took me watching you walk out of my life to realize that you were more than just a part of my life. You were a person who had been this amazing, outspoken, creative and independent soul when I fell in love with you, and I had crushed that by letting my high falutin ways become our life."

I had to giggle a little. "High falutin?" I gave him an innocent smile and he returned it.

"I mean it. I guess I just thought we would get through all of the bumps in the road and we would live the life my parents had, or the life that my co-workers do, and that would be enough. But I never wanted that kind of life, and that is the whole reason I fell in love with you in the first place. You were nothing like them, and I forced you to play the role of happy housewife when you had your own dreams pushed aside. I am so grateful for you being strong enough to walk out on me, even though it was the most devastating moment of my life, because it made me see who you had been before. And that was the girl I was in love with." He took a long pause and sighed before he looked me right in the face and said, "The girl I am still in love with."

And now those beautiful piercing eyes were once again invading my soul. He had said some incredibly serious things, things I had felt myself but wasn't quite sure I would ever hear from him. Things I didn't even know I was ready to hear from him.

I stared at him for what seemed like ages, and he stared at me. He took a few deep breaths, but I don't think I could even force myself to take a breath. I didn't know what to say, or do, so I just sat there and stared at him.

Finally, he broke the silence.

"Emmie, I know you made your choice, and I will try and respect that, but I just want to know if there is any part of you that feels like maybe we could…"

At that very moment, Miss Rainbow Sunshine herself came over to our table and said, "Are you two ready to order now?"

I almost threw up.

I couldn't sit there any longer. I stood up, bumping into the table as I pushed out of my chair and said "Excuse me. I need to use the restroom."

I practically ran through the maze of tables and flung myself into the ladies bathroom door, praying I would be alone once inside. I never looked back to see if anyone was staring at me, but I knew at least one person probably was.

I went to the sink and immediately splashed cold water on my face.

What the hell had just happened?

I mean, I knew Charlie was a little bit of a mess and who doesn't want an amazing man like him still pining after them, but what was happening to *me?* Why was I feeling like a giddy school girl again?

I thought I was through this. I thought I was over Charlie-ok maybe not over him but I had made my choice to leave. Hadn't I moved on? I knew we both were in different places of our lives, and that he was Fifth Avenue, and I was apparently So Ho. So, why was he saying the most amazing things to me? What was he thinking? And what was he going to ask me if I had stayed there?

Oh my God, I was in a restaurant, yet again, and Charlie was asking me questions I didn't know how to answer, again.

But unlike last time, I wasn't feeling like running away. Why didn't I want to run away? Did I want this? Did I want Charlie back in my life? Or was I just lonely?

He was the man of my dreams, and those dreams were so good most of the time. Sure, we had differences, but with everything he had just said to me, maybe we could work through all of that and find our happily ever after again. If we both understood each other, what was stopping us from having it all?

Whatever the case, I couldn't stay in this bathroom forever. Could I? I owed it to him to at least talk about this, right?

I looked at myself in the mirror, and I didn't look the same as I did when I left my room this morning. I was flustered yes, but I was scared when I had come here, not knowing how the day would go or if Charlie and I would get into a fight. And now that I *knew* how the day was going, and that Charlie didn't come here to fight, or to gain closure, but to tell me he might possibly want me back? Why wasn't I scared anymore?

I wiped the water from my face, straightened my shoulders and tried to at least look like I was allowed to be out in the world.

I wasn't quite sure what I was going to say, but I knew I wasn't going to run out on Charlie again. I pushed the door to the restroom open and expected to see him still sitting at the table. Instead, I saw our lovely waitress with the rainbow hair awkwardly standing over his empty chair, waiting for me to return.

"Um, he told me to give this to you." She handed me a napkin that had just a few tiny words written on it.

Before I could focus my eyes to read what he had written for me, she had gone and apparently hidden in the back of the restaurant. I assumed the note said something like, "thanks for nothing" or "don't ever talk to me again." Definitely something with a little more bite. I deserved something nasty from him. I had left him at a restaurant, waiting with his heart on the table, not once but twice. To my surprise, the note simply said, "Talk to your heart and call me."

So, he was really asking me back into his life? I felt so happy, and confused, and completely torn.

Just this morning, I had decided I was starting my life over alone. I was going to try and mend my broken fences, but I was going to move on and find out where I was in my life. It was going to be a rough road, but I needed to find out what I wanted, and who I wanted. And it seemed easy enough this morning when I was alone anyway. Neither man was in my life so of course it was easy to say that I could do it alone. Did I have any other choice?

But now I was being given an invitation back into Charlie's life. Back to the easy and comfortable life I had been living for most of my adult life thus far. It seemed so tempting. No, it was more than tempting. As I said, I felt happy.

It felt as if a few lifetimes had passed within the short time since Charlie had asked me to marry him. So much had happened, so many feelings had changed and then changed again. My head was reeling and my heart felt like it could beat right out of my chest.

Maybe this was how it was all supposed to pan out. Maybe our non-proposal, me walking out and running to

Jackson and then walking out on him, maybe that was all just bringing me back to Charlie.

And now that he believed in me, and understood that I needed to have my art and a career, maybe it would all work out this time and we could have our fairy tale that I had always imagined.

I made up my mind right then and there.

Yes, this was going to work.

This was exactly what I needed and I was going to have it.

I didn't order any food, and Charlie had already left a fifty dollar bill on the table for our drinks. Perhaps enduring our awkward meeting was worth it for the rainbow-haired waitress after all. I picked up my stuff and quickly headed out. I was going to find Charlie and tell him I was ready and he was what I wanted.

With a much bigger than usual smile on my face, I almost ran out the door thinking about how happy we were going to be. It was because of that, my mind wasn't aware that someone else was coming through the door at the same time.

I slammed into the extremely familiar and sweet smelling shoulder of the man I had finally managed to stop thinking about for the past few moments.

Chapter 10.....

"Emmie." Jackson's voice almost scared me. He was the absolute last person I had expected to see right now. "Fancy running into you." He sounded as nonchalant as he always did.

"Oh my God, Jackson! What are you doing here?" I was also trying to sound cool but it came out more like an accusation.

He stepped back as if my words stung a little and pointed to the picture of a gigantic, steaming cup of coffee on the window, "Coffee." And then there was his crooked smile. "I guess more importantly my question would be, what are *you* doing here? I guess a lot can happen in a few days, like you suddenly acquiring a taste for coffee."

"Oh, no, no I still hate the stuff. I uh, I was just..." Crap. I didn't even know what I could tell him at this point.

Should I say I was meeting someone? No, that would sound like a date. And I definitely couldn't tell him I was meeting Charlie because I wasn't in the mood to have another fight with him. I was trying to mend fences.

It was so great to see him. I had almost forgotten how much I had truly missed seeing his face. "I was going to get some food but..."

"But, you forgot?" He finally smiled a real Jackson smile. I forgot what that smile did to me. On top of the butterflies I was also speechless.

I was hoping that he would say something, anything, so that I had a few minutes to procure something for my own mouth to say, but he just stood there in the doorway and stared at me with a raised eyebrow and his devastatingly handsome half-grin. With Jackson, it was never as easy as I wished it would be.

"Well, I was going to get some food but then I realized I had some place I needed to be." Ominous and yet it still worked.

"Well, don't let me keep you from anything." He said as he slid in the door and moved to the side. "I guess we can have a cup of conversation another time."

He casually strolled to the counter as if he had just bumped into a stranger, not someone he had just lived with. I felt a little dejected but I knew it was just a wall he had put up. And as unprepared as I was for this chance encounter, I wasn't about to let him get away from me that easily. I had been trying to talk to him for almost a week now and he hadn't returned any of my calls. It was now or never and I refused to let never be where our story ended.

"I am sure that my, uh, meeting can wait just a little bit." I said as I followed him to the counter. He didn't turn around to acknowledge me, but I swear I could see the hint of a smile on his turned away cheeks.

"Yes, could I have a large coffee with two sugars and two creams?" he asked the rainbow haired girl behind the counter.

She was staring at me with a confused look on her face and I don't think she realized that Jackson had even said a word to her.

When she made no attempt to move, he looked back at me, seeing that she was staring and said, "Did you want anything?"

I barely even touched the drink I had while I was with Charlie, and I could see that it was still on the table where we were sitting. I looked back at it and said, "Um, I will just have my drink over there I guess."

The waitress just rolled her eyes and looked up at Jackson. She had a devious grin on her face, as if she knew that this was another man I would quite possibly run out on as well. I guess I would be her entertainment for the day.

"Should I bring you something to her table?" she asked in a bitter sweet acid tone.

Jackson shrugged his shoulders at me and said, "So, you have a table? Am I allowed to join you at *your* table?"

There was always a hint of sarcasm to Jackson, but I could tell he was wondering what I was up to. Too bad I had no intentions of telling him why I had a table and what had happened the five minutes before he had walked in.

"Oh I think she just meant because I was going to sit down at that table but I decided not to." Yeah, that sounded plausible.

Before any other feet could get planted in or around my mouth, I quickly sat down and pulled out a chair for him.

He sat down and bit his lower lip, looking very uncomfortable. Very un-Jackson-like.

"So, I have been meaning to call you back. But it's been a very busy time for me since you left." The last word lingered on his lips as if he was pained by it. Was he really upset that I left? I couldn't have guessed, it was almost as if he fell off the face of the Earth.

"Ya' know, you really didn't have to move out just because we had one little fight Emmie."

He took a long awkward pause and just stared at a spot on the table that was wearing away. He started picking at it and maintained his silence. I wasn't sure if I was supposed to say something but, as per my usual bewildered attitude around Jackson, I was speechless. This would make the second time today I had no words for the man sitting across this table from me.

Finally he looked up at me and I didn't recognize the look on his face. He was normally so cocky and bold, like I could say anything to him and it would just roll right off his shoulders like rain on a rooftop. This was not that face.

"No, it wasn't like that, I just..." I had practiced what I was going to say a thousand times for when he finally answered my calls, but my confidence just seemed to falter seeing him so vulnerable. "Jackson, I said a lot of things. Things that I wish I hadn't said."

"Yeah yeah, we both said some stuff. Like I said, it was a fight. And not a very productive one by the way. I remember having knock-down brawls with Amber that ended with a lot more broken glass and a lot less clothing." A smile crept on his lips as he imagined God knows what.

"But then again, we haven't gotten to the make-up part of our fight yet, have we?"

Whoa.

I was not expecting him to be flirty.

I was also not expecting to feel things about him being flirty. My mind started going places it probably shouldn't have while being in a public place.

He must've seen he had made me uncomfortable, although I don't think he knew in what way because he quickly put his hand up and said, "Relax Emmie, I was just messing around with you. Trying to lighten the mood."

The waitress brought him his coffee and he nodded his head to her in gratitude as he tipped it into his mouth. I couldn't help but watch that cup touching his lips and feeling a slight twinge of jealousy wishing I were that coffee.

"Anyway, as I was saying, it was just a fight. Tempers flare, words are said, blah blah blah. The point is, it was nothing to move out over. So, whenever you are ready to come back, you are welcome to."

Now, he said this with all the confidence in the world, but he never quite looked me in the eyes as he always did. He just started picking at the top of his coffee cup. I don't really know if he meant those words, or if he had rehearsed them or what, but it felt like he was asking a question rather than stating a point.

"Jack, you know I didn't just move out because of our fight, right? I mean, I know I said a lot of things that were a little harsh, but I, well I meant most of them." I meant them, didn't I?

"Oh." He said, rolling his cup over in his hands and staring at it. Then he nodded his head at me in a strange unfamiliar gesture. "Okay then."

"No, I mean, I didn't *mean* them, I just meant that I just wasn't quite sure what it was that we were doing. I was just crashing at your place until I found a place, wasn't I?"

He looked at me a little confused and opened his mouth as if he was going to say something, but then shut it again. He thought for a few seconds and then in a small voice said, "Well, I guess maybe at first it was like that, but..." he quickly took a sip of his coffee, which dribbled out of the side of his mouth onto his lap and made his whole body flinch. "Ahem, hmmmm." He cleared his throat. "But things changed, or at least they did for me, Emmie."

Ok, I really wasn't expecting that. He was being entirely sincere and now he was looking at me, I guess expecting me to say that things had changed for me as well. Had they?

I didn't know what to say. I mean, yes things definitely had changed between us since I had moved in. We had become so much closer, and it was really nice. But I had never actually sat down and thought about why it felt so nice. I had been so wrapped up in all of the Charlie drama.

"Emmie, I haven't been returning your calls because I was embarrassed at how stupid I was acting, about everything. And I don't just mean about our little fight. I didn't exactly know how to say I was sorry, so I figured radio silence was better than saying another stupid thing."

"What do you mean?" Why was he apologizing to me? Why were both of these men in my life (or not in my life) apologizing to me? Maybe I was mistaken here, but wasn't I the bad guy?

"I didn't expect things to move as fast as they did, but if we are being honest here, I have been attracted to you since I first saw you on that street corner."

Now was my turn to sit there open-mouthed and speechless. It was a face I knew quite well these days. Men just seemed to keep surprising me at every turn. Thankfully, little Miss Rainbow Hair had perfect timing as usual.

"You two need refills?" She asked with what I would have to describe as the hugest smirk on her face. She was holding a pot of coffee so obviously she didn't mean me, not to mention the fact that I hadn't even touched my tea since I had sat down with Charlie.

And with that, my mind went back to Charlie. Charlie whom just a few moments ago had asked me back into his life and whom I was running off to right before running into Jackson. This day was just getting better and better wasn't it?

"I could definitely use a top-off," Jackson said and downed the entire cup of coffee he had been holding.

Rainbow Bright poured some steaming coffee into his cup and looked at me, still grinning, "And how are you doin'?"

She looked down at my full cup and I knew she wasn't asking about my liquid requirements.

"Yeah, I'm good thanks." I couldn't stop the attitude in my voice. I wasn't exactly happy about my love life, or lack thereof, being her entertainment for the afternoon. Not that there was anything I could do about it.

"Well, I'm over there if you need anything" she smiled at Jackson and rolled her eyes at me. Then her and her hot pot of coffee walked back to the counter where she proceeded to stare in our direction.

"Friendly girl." Jackson said with raised eyebrows.

"Yeah, she's a real ray of sunshine that one." I rolled my own eyes.

"Well, she makes a very decent cup of coffee, and I kind of like her hair." Jackson said in a really Jackson sort of way.

"But as I was saying, I wanted to apologize for acting like an idiot. I know you didn't come to my place looking for…well, actually I am not really sure why you came to my place that night. You could've gone to a hotel or a girlfriend's house or something. I guess I just told myself you came to me because you felt the same things I had been feeling." He took another sip of his coffee and burned his tongue.

"Ouch!" he quickly put the cup down and I heard the waitress snickering behind him. I shot her the dirtiest look I could muster and she turned around and hurried into the kitchen.

"Are you ok?" I said, offering up my napkin to clean up the mess the hot coffee had made when it spilled out of his mouth.

"Yeah, yeah, didn't burn my tongue as bad as the last time." He wiped his mouth and reached for his cup absentmindedly to take another sip. Quickly he remembered and put it back down. "I wonder why it is that I always seem to get burned when you are around?" His whole face turned into a devious grin, and then he chuckled to himself. I however did not find it as amusing.

"Hey, it's not my fault you don't blow on things before you put them in your mouth!"

He looked around as if addressing the whole coffee shop and pointed at me, saying, "Oooh, excuse me folks, I'm sorry about this one, she's got such a potty mouth!"

"Stop it!" I said, hitting him on the arm as I laughed harder than I probably should have. "You are embarrassing me!"

"I'm not the one talking about putting hot things in my mouth, Emmie. I mean, really, what would your mother think about that kind of talk? Good heavens child!!" He said in a high pitched southern accent and placed the back of his hand on his forehead as if he was about to faint.

We both just started laughing out loud, loud enough that everyone in there was starting to stare at us, but it didn't matter. It was so good to laugh with him again. I was realizing how much I had truly missed this Jackson. This flirty, cocky, deliciously handsome Jackson. We always just clicked. And for some reason, I never seemed to feel embarrassed or incompetent or small when I was with him.

After the laughing was officially over, an awkward moment of silence loomed between us and he once again reached for his coffee. This time, he took a moment to blow on the top and he lifted his eyebrow and grinned at me before taking a sip.

I wanted to be the one to say something next so I decided it would be best to do it while he had coffee in his mouth.

"Jackson, if anyone should be apologizing, it is me." I took a long deep breath before finishing what I had wanted to say to him all week.

"I know that it was wrong of me to come to you that night that Charlie and I broke things off. I honestly didn't even know where I was going when I left, but something just pulled me to you. And I don't really know what that means, but it wasn't fair to you that I wound up on your doorstep and expected you to pick up my broken pieces."

He was finished his sip but he hadn't yet put his cup back on the table. He was looking at me and turning it in his palms.

"I moved out, not because we had that fight, but because I realized I needed to start acting like a big girl and take care of myself for a change."

"Emmie, it was nice to be able to help you."

"Please don't misunderstand me, I will forever be grateful for everything you…"

"Let's not get into this again Em, I'm not looking for your gratitude here. What I was trying to say before was that ever since that first time we talked, I started to have these feelings. I mean, I didn't really know what I was feeling, but I knew that I felt more for you that first day then I had for Amber the whole time we were together. And I liked it, I liked you."

Oh no.

Those were words I had wanted him to say for a while; at least I think I wanted him to say them. Yes, I think I did. But what about Charlie?

I had no idea what I wanted, or needed, or should do.

"Ok, so this is me, putting myself out there, and believe me Em, I have wanted to say this for so long but you seemed pretty into that Charlie guy and I never really thought I stood much of a chance with you."

He thought *he* never stood a chance with *me*?

"It's just that having you there in the apartment, in my apartment, it felt so nice. Being able to come home to someone who didn't want to fight with me, or just have sex with me. Well, don't get me wrong, the sex part wasn't something I ever felt too bad about. That was pretty good, very good actually, but…"

"That is definitely something I didn't need to know."

"I'm sorry. I just meant that with Amber we didn't have much of a relationship. We didn't talk about anything that mattered, we didn't laugh together, it was just a *use me I'll use you* kinda thing. And I thought I was cool with that, for a while. And then I met you, and I had never clicked like that with someone before."

He paused and raked his hand through his smooth messy hair.

"God, I sound like a woman here! Are you going to chime in and tell me I'm crazy or go to Hell or anything to shut me up? You can just put me out of my misery, go on, get it over with. Just tell me you don't feel the same way about me and I should grow a set."

I sat there, almost completely stunned into silence. Here I thought my life was becoming less confusing and complicated today and I had just tangled myself into a web where two ridiculously handsome spiders were telling me how tasty I looked.

I honestly had no idea what to do or say to him. And although I thought I knew what I was going to say to Charlie just a few moments ago, that had just changed when Jackson told me that he had feelings for me.

But why would that have changed anything with Charlie? I wasn't one hundred percent sure but I thought it was because Jackson was right. We clicked. But did that mean I was supposed to give up my fairy tale with Charlie because I had a few laughs with Jackson? What if we clicked as friends but nothing else? And Charlie and I clicked too, it was just a different kind of clicking. Ugh! What was wrong with me? Could it be possible to be completely in love with two different men at the same time?

It wasn't something you ever heard about in the fairy tales. The princess was only lucky enough to have one prince Charming to ride off into the sunset with, wasn't she?

The only thing I was certain about right now was that I needed time. Time to think about what I wanted in my life. What I needed in my life, or more importantly who I needed.

I had to get out of there without saying anything that could hurt Jackson.

My "fairy godmother" must have been listening to me at that very moment because just as I was about to open my mouth, my phone rang. It was Gina from the shop.

"I'm sorry Jackson, I have to get this, excuse me for a moment?" I said as I stood up and walked to the back of the coffee shop to answer the call.

"Hello."

"Emmie, thank God I reached you!" She sounded out of breath.

"What is it Gina, is something wrong?" I said. Oh God, had something terrible happened? Was there a robbery? Or something worse, like a fire? "Did something happen at the shop?"

"Ha! Did something happen?" she exclaimed. "Yeah something happened! Some guy just came in and bought all of the sample pieces you had in the case and he said he wanted more! He handed me five hundred bucks and when I told him I didn't have change for that kinda money he said just keep it! You've gotta come back here and give me more stuff! I tell you what kid, if this is what we can expect outta you, you just may be my favorite new person!"

For some reason, my stomach plunged into my throat. I should've been happy, but I feared that I knew what had happened.

"What did the guy look like?" I asked, hoping beyond hope I was wrong.

"Oh, he was straight up Fifth Avenue. Pin-striped black suit, probably like Armani or something fancy~schmancy like that. And a gold watch as big as my head. Oh and he was quite a looker too, I tell ya, if Johnny wasn't already taking care of my business, I woulda been asking this guy to ring my bell! Aint that right, Shirley?"

I heard the other girl who worked part time in the shop say "Uh-huh, that's right Gina!" and they both started laughing.

172

I wasn't in the mood to laugh. I was actually rather mad. You wouldn't think a normal person would get mad at someone buying all of their stuff, I mean, I wanted it to sell and for people to like it. That was the whole point. But when that someone was Charlie, and I knew that it was, it meant that there was an ulterior motive behind it. And I thought we had finally gotten past all of that.

"Gina, thanks for calling me. I will be right there, I'm just a couple blocks away. Give me fifteen minutes, ok?" I tried to sound happy, but I wasn't very good at hiding my emotions when they were on the verge of popping out of my head.

I hung up the phone and went back over to the table where Jackson was drinking the rest of his coffee. I picked up my sweet tea, the tea that had survived two declarations of love already today and poured it down my throat in one giant gulp.

"Whoa! Take it easy!" Jackson said. "What did that tea ever do to you?" He smiled back at me and I felt my knees buckle a little.

"I'm sorry Jack. There's an emergency at the shop and Gina needs me right away." It was mostly the truth. And a good excuse for not having to finish this conversation right now.

"Is everything ok? I could walk you, or…"

"No, no, everything is fine. And I don't want to take you away from your drink. I know how men feel about their coffee." I tried to muster up a casual smile so that he wouldn't ask any more questions. "Um, can we finish this conversation another time?"

"Well, I hope so, and soon Em." He didn't sound as casual as I was trying to be.

"Yes, yes, we need to talk soon. I just really have to go, I'm sorry." Still clutching my cup in my hands, I started to head for the door. I glanced over my shoulder at Jackson sitting there, looking a little stunned, and a little like a lost puppy. I called back at him, "Can I call you tomorrow, and will you answer this time?" I gave him a quick coy smile.

He answered with another smile, "Yes, if you call, I will answer Emmie."

Chapter 11.....

I ran out the door, feeling a little better. I would have
tonight to think about things and I would call him
tomorrow. For now, I would have to deal with this whole
Charlie situation.

I couldn't believe he had just left here and went straight
to the shop, without even telling me he was going there. And
then to just buy all my stuff like that! It was ridiculous! I
didn't need his charity! That was the whole point, I wanted

to stand on my own two feet, and I thought he finally got that.

I barely remembered walking to the shop. My mind had been racing the whole time. When I walked in, all three girls were behind the counter and they started clapping when I came through the door.

"There she is! Our super star!" Gina yelled and the other two girls hooped and hollered.

"Oh stop it! It's not what you think." I said, blushing.

"What I think is that you just made some cold hard cash today, and now I'm not feeling so bad about taking only a five percent cut. I wonder what I will do with all that moolah."

"You should probably go get that lip waxed Gin, you're starting to look like your Uncle Joey!" Shirley teased and started cackling to herself.

Gina grabbed a stack of papers and whacked Shirley over the head with them playfully. "You are one to talk about facial hair Shirls, I seem to recall you needin' a weed whacker to tame that caterpillar you call an eyebrow." She put her index finger across her forehead to mimic a uni-brow.

"Anyway, Emmie. I was a little worried about you, what with not knowing you from Adam and all. But I am very glad we decided to bring you in here. And I think we need to celebrate."

"Yeah, woo-hoo! Margarita Monday!!" Laura, the young girl I had met on my first venture into the shop, threw her arms in the air.

"I don't know about all that Laura. The last time we tried to have Margarita Monday, we didn't see you until Thursday." Gina said.

"Yeah but that's just because you didn't feed me first. You're gonna have to spring for a couple appy's before you give me any alcohol. You know there is a delicate balance between nourishing the body and flooding the soul."

"Well, little miss zen garden, I don't think it matters how many plates of onion rings you put in there first, 8 margaritas could flood the alley behind the shop." They all laughed. "So, what do ya say Emmie? You up for a night out on the town?" Gina raised her eyebrows at me.

"Come on! We can show you exactly what you were missin' up there on Fifth Avenue." Laura said as she ran over to me and linked her arm in mine.

"Well, to be honest, I could really use a girl's night out right about now." I was so angry with Charlie, and confused about my recently surfaced feelings for Jackson.

"It's settled then! Drinks on the boss lady!!" Laura shouted as she skipped upstairs with me attached to her. "First we gotta get you out of that horrid outfit and into some dancing clothes."

"I don't really have any gowns here…"

"Oh no, I don't mean fancy dancing. I'm talkin' about clubbin' girl! Are you telling me you aint never been clubbing? Wow! We have gotta work on that. I know exactly what we need. You go in there and change out of that mess and I will bring you up something more suitable for where we are going tonight." She pushed me into my room and ran back down the stairs.

I called after her, "Where are we going?" but she had already made her way into the shop again. I was kind of afraid, but also very excited. I had never really had much of an adult girl's night out. I mean, back in high school, me and Amy would have sleep-overs, but they never included alcohol, unless you count the times we would try and sneak a beer out of her dad's fridge. And I doubt tonight would be ending with us doing our nails over an empty box of pizza and talking about how Mitch Stewart was staring at my boobs in gym class. Well, I didn't *think* it would end like that, but who knew?

When she came back, Laura was holding two tiny pieces of black fabric that looked like maybe they would fit on a small dog, not over my body.

"*What* is *that?*" I asked, trying to figure out which piece went where.

"Hey now, don't go getting your panties in a bunch. I know you usually dress a little more uptight, but this my dear, is smokin' hot! Here, try it on."

She flung the tiny scraps at me and I flipped them over a few times, trying to find a tag or something to give me a clue as to which end was up and what covered what on my body.

After a few confused moments, she grabbed them back out of my hands and placed them against my body. I still wasn't sure how I was   supposed to shove all that God had given me into those tiny little sacks, but with a little help from my friend, I managed to cover just slightly less than a bathing suit would.

"Damn girl, look at yourself! Now that's what I'm talkin' about!" she said as she angled me towards the mirror.

One look and I was mortified! "Oh no, no, no, no! I can't go out in this! Laura, seriously, I look like pretty woman before she got *un-prostituted.*"

"Yeah! That's who I was thinking of! Anyway, you look gorgeous and besides, if you wear something from your closet to where we are going, you might as well just spray man repellant all over yourself."

I'm actually ok with that though, I'm not looking for a..."

"Don't you even say you aren't looking for a man, because we all know that every woman is looking for a man, even after she finds a man. Then she is just looking for a better man."

She quickly got changed into a dress that actually covered even less than mine (so I guess I was wearing her conservative outfit) and said, "Hey, could I borrow one of your necklaces?"

Despite how embarrassed I felt in that getup, I couldn't help but smile that she had asked if she could wear my jewelry.

"Yeah, of course." I said and pulled out the drawer where I had stashed a bunch of things I recently put together. I found a short black beaded one and held it out to her. "This will match just about anything, plus you will still be able to dance to your hearts content."

She shook her head at me. "I swear, we gotta work on your accent if you are gonna be a New Yorker. But this…" she said as she pointed to the necklace, "is fab-u-lous." After clasping it around her neck and doing a couple test dance moves, she seemed very pleased.

"Ok, so are you ready for a night you will never forget?"

I looked at myself one last time in the mirror, in an outfit I wouldn't have even felt comfortable going to sleep in, and decided what the hell. You really only live once, and I wanted to forget about the decisions I so desperately needed to make, just for a little while.

"Absolutely."

When we got to the club, I felt more out of my element than ever before. There were so many scantily clad people smashed together dancing (if you can call rubbing every inch of your body against someone else's dancing) and the music was so loud I couldn't hear myself think. Maybe that wouldn't be a bad thing though.

Laura immediately started dancing as soon as we walked through the door and dragged me with her over to the bar. She pushed her way through about six very large men in velour suits who were more than happy to have us slide past them.

"Ladies, how we doin' tonight?" One of the younger guys yelled in my ear. He reeked of body spray and hair gel, and I was a little scared to make eye contact with him but thankfully Laura just shoved him to the side.

"No thanks Eddie, we aren't really looking to get crabs tonight."

"Hey, hey babe, that's harsh. You know it was just the one time and I got the medicine right away." He said as he smiled and chugged his beer.

"Come on beautiful. You and me could be great together." He started to put his arm around me but Laura shook him off.

"Don't even talk to him Emmie, he is disgusting. Last month, I had one too many mojitos and wound up in the slimy sheets of hell next to this dirt bag." She poked him in the chest and grabbed my arm. "Never gonna happen again Eddie."

"Suit yourself. But if your lovely friend here wants to take a ride on the E train," he ran his hand all the way down his chest, "just come and find me. The train runs all night long." He grabbed a new beer off the bar and danced his way into the crowd.

"Yeah, and you will be running all the way to the doctor if you make that mistake." She yelled in my ear. "Now let's go get a drink before he comes back."

She bought me a beer and as she handed it to me I realized I had never had an actual beer at an actual bar. Before I met Charlie, I was so young and never really went out to bars. And he never took me anywhere that didn't force you into a $300 bottle of wine. I just stared at it for a few seconds until she gave me a look.

"You too good for beer?"

"Oh, no." I didn't want to tell her I was such a loser that I had never had a beer in a bar before. "It's just not my usual brand."

"They don't have a big variety of stuff here so it's either this or a tequila shot." She didn't wait for an answer, just shoved it in my hand and pulled me out to the dance floor.

I wasn't sure what to do at first, so I just followed Laura's lead. She was surprisingly limber and obviously didn't share my incessant fear of embarrassing myself in public. After a few beers, it became much easier to let go of my inhibitions and I found myself dancing around a few random guys. It's amazing how men will flock to two girls dancing, especially if they are wearing clothes that looked more like underwear than the real thing.

Gina and Shirley were on the other side of the dance floor leaning against the bar. I nodded my head at them and continued to dance. It felt so freeing to just put all of the drama of the past few weeks into a corner of my mind.

I would have to deal with it later, the whole Charlie wanting me back, and then buying all of my jewelry, Jackson shutting me out and then professing his feelings for me. It was a mess. But with the music playing and my body just moving in ways it has never moved before, I felt like nothing could bring me down.

I was finally starting to let loose and have a good time. I understood why people did this. I even forgot about how I was dressed and just marveled at how good I felt in my own skin. As cliché as it sounds, I almost felt like I could fly.

But, as all good pilots will tell you, you gotta keep your eyes on the skies. So, while I was enjoying the uncomplicated air, things took a nosedive when someone grabbed my arm. I turned around and found myself staring into the familiar eyes of Charlie. So much for forgetting about my troubles for the night.

"What in the world are you doing here Charlie??" I asked, not really looking forward to that answer. I didn't know if I was happy to see him or not, but he didn't look very pleased to see me.

"Well, to be honest, I talked to your boss and she mentioned that you might be coming here tonight, and I really couldn't wait to see you again. I guess I thought I would be hearing from you already."

When had he talked to my boss? Oh yeah, probably when he was buying all my jewelry and making me feel like an idiot. His demeanor had done a complete one eighty since this afternoon at the café. He sounded angry, and I immediately felt like a child that was about to be scolded, even though I was unsure what I did wrong.

"I had, well, I *have* a lot to think about."

"It doesn't really look like you are doing much thinking." He said as he eyed up my ensemble with a chuckle. "What is this, Halloween? I mean, Emmie, this really is not you."

Even though he was laughing, I could almost taste his disgust. Was it what I was wearing, or this place? It wasn't *that* bad. I mean, I knew he had been born with a silver spoon in his mouth, but he had never acted like such a snob before. And he also had never made me feel so low.

"Well, actually Charlie, I don't know that you really know who I am anymore. I'm not quite sure you ever really did in the first place."

"What are you talking about? Of course I know you. Are you telling me you've always had some burning desire to dress like a hooker and go prancing around in skeevy clubs while working class men fight over who gets to buy you a $3 beer? Come on, I thought you were better than that Emmie."

Wow.

I was in complete shock. He had never acted like this before. Even on his worst day, he wouldn't have talked to me like that. What had happened to him?

The look on my face must have said it all because he immediately grabbed my arm and said, "Hey, I just meant that this isn't you. You are an amazing, smart, capable woman and you don't need to demean yourself by showing your body to every person who walks into this place."

"Um, Charlie, I think maybe you should go."

"No Em, wait, I just, I really want to talk to you, and I don't want to do it here. And I don't want to do it while other guys are staring at you the way all of these guys are. I've had a rough week and I just want to get things back to normal. Can we just go somewhere?"

"Em, is this guy bothering you?" Laura said as she looked Charlie up and down. He was dressed in the same suit he had on earlier but now instead of looking like a sophisticated businessman, he just stood out like a sore thumb.

"No, this is my, um…"I wasn't sure what to call him, since he wasn't my boyfriend anymore, and right now he wasn't even acting like my friend. "Well, why am I introducing? You two have already met haven't you?" I said, backing away from Charlie's grasp.

"What do you mean? I have never seen this girl before in my life."

"Oh, you mean you are telling me that you didn't go to my shop today and buy out all of my jewelry?"

Charlie's face turned a little red and he looked away from me like he always did when he was uncomfortable. "Emmie, I.."

"What were you thinking Charlie? That one day I wouldn't wonder how all of my stuff just happened to wind up in your sock drawer? Or were you planning on just throwing it out?" I could feel my cheeks getting warm the angrier I got. "That's it, isn't it? I mean, it's all just junk to you anyway."

"No, that's not true. Listen, I just wanted to show you how much I support what you are doing. I wasn't trying to make you feel bad. I thought I was doing exactly the opposite. Don't you want your stuff to sell? I thought that was the whole point of you being in that place instead of home with me."

With that he grabbed my arms and tried to pull me closer to him, but I jerked away and flung myself back into one of the velour suit posse who happily caught me in his arms and didn't seem to want to let me go.

Charlie pulled me back towards him and gave the guy a look of disgust. "Excuse me, would you mind letting go of my girlfriend?"

"Whoa. Seriously. What has come over you in the past few hours? Weren't we just talking about how you regretted the things you did while we were together and how you wanted to make it up to me?"

"I do Emmie, I want you to come home with me. We can talk about this there. I don't want to make a huge scene at a place like this. You know the ladies at bridge club would have my head on a stick for even being seen in this place."

"Do you think I give a rat's ass what the ladies at the bridge club think? They never believed I was good enough for you, and I've always wondered if you felt the same way. I believe now I have my answer. No one is stopping you from leaving, and in fact, no one even asked you to come. I can't believe I thought things were different, I thought we could go back and that everything would be perfect. I was willing to forgive you for everything that happened..."

"Everything that happened?" His voice rose to an angry tone I had never heard before. "Emmie, you left me sitting in my favorite restaurant with an engagement ring in my hand and went and shacked up with some guy. I would say it is *you* who needs the forgiveness, wouldn't you agree?"

I could tell almost immediately regretted saying that because he sighed and his voice became gentle again. "I mean, it's just that you really hurt me and if I can get past all of that, then we should have a chance to move on. Don't you think we deserve another shot, Emmie? You said it yourself; you were coming back to me. Are you really telling me that just because I bought some of your jewelry to show my support and love for you that I deserve to be punished? I love you Emmie, and I know you still love me. Isn't that worth fighting for?"

I didn't even know what to say. I did still love him. And what he had done wasn't an unforgivable act. It wasn't like he had cheated on me or anything. Maybe he was just trying to show me that he supports my decisions?

Most of what he was saying was right. He was just saying it all wrong. Horribly, horribly wrong. And right now, I couldn't even look at him.

"Charlie, I really think you should go. I need to clear my head and think about everything."

"Please Emmie, come home with me. You can think about all of this in our apartment, in our bed. I don't want you staying with that guy anymore. I let you play house for long enough with that...*boy*. I mean, I'm not going to judge you, you were upset and you just made a bad decision but you need to come home."

Ok, now I was confused.

"What are you even talking about Charlie? Playing house? I'm staying at the shop." He couldn't have possibly known about Jackson, I never said a word about where I was, just that I was staying with a friend.

"Oh come on Emmie, I know you have been sleeping with that artist guy down in SoHo. Don't try to deny it. Brian saw the two of you parading around town just a few days after you left me. And like I said I am willing to forgive you for that, if you would just come home."

Oh my God. Charlie knew I was with Jackson this whole time? I was mortified, and yet still very, very angry with him.

"Listen, I *am* staying at the shop now, but it wasn't like that at all Charlie."

"I don't even care. We were in a bad place and you needed to get that out of your system. I understand that, believe me, I totally understand. But let's be real here. You can't have a future with that guy. You belong with me, just like I belong with you."

"First of all, nothing happened between me and Jackson. Nothing." That was a slight exaggeration, but technically nothing physical had happened. Honestly, I wasn't even sure what had happened, but definitely nothing physical.

"And secondly, what do you mean 'believe me I know'? Did you, I mean, have you ever been with someone else while we were together?" I felt my chest tightening. "Oh my God, did you cheat on me Charlie?"

"Emmie, it's not like that, I just meant that sometimes things with us got a little heated and I needed to go let off some steam. It doesn't mean anything. Just like I know this guy doesn't mean anything to you. Because you love me."

At that moment, I could've sworn the music stopped and the ground shifted under my feet. Everything started to blur together and I knew it wasn't just the alcohol. Charlie had cheated on me. And it was obvious it hadn't happened just once.

"Emmie?" He reached for my arm again and I stumbled backward until I was against the bar. "Please Emmie, let's go home and talk."

I couldn't even bring myself to speak, so I just shook my head. Fairy tales didn't have cheaters in them. The prince didn't skirt around behind the princesses back when they had an argument. I had to get out of here, and I needed to get as far away from Charlie as possible.

I turned around and started heading for the door.

"Emmie. Emmie!" Charlie called after me but I was able to maneuver through the crowd much better than he was. Being small always had its advantages.

I pushed open the door to the club and sucked in some of the cool night air. It was not yet spring but it was unseasonably warm for this time of year and I was so thankful for that, due to my lack of a jacket, or a dress that actually covered anything.

The door opened behind me and I was ready to run away again from Charlie, but it was Laura and Gina who had witnessed that whole scene.

"Oh my God Em, that was crazy!" Laura said.

"Yeah, if I had any idea who that guy was, or what he had done to you, I would've thrown his money back in his face."

Just then Shirley pushed herself out the door behind them. "Yeah right, you still would've taken his money. You just would've sent him on his way with a black eye."

All three of them huddled around me.

"Are you ok sweetie?" Gina asked.

"Yes. Well, no, not really. I kinda just wanna go home." I said, shivering a little from the cold, and maybe from other things.

"Sure, let's go pay our tab and we will walk you."

"Hey Gina, you think I could get a beer to go?" Laura called after her. "It's not like you offer to pick up the tab often."

The two of them ran back inside while I waited on the curb with Shirley. We didn't say anything to each other, and no one said much on the way home either. I am glad they didn't ask me to explain because I was still reeling.

None of that really just happened, did it?

One minute I was having an amazing time dancing, and the next I was running away from Charlie, my prince, who had just told me in not so many words that he had cheated on me.

Chapter 12.....

Laura and Shirley lived in the same building, just a block away, so Gina and I said our goodbyes to them and headed off towards the shop.

As we rounded the corner, I saw a dark figure sitting on the front steps and cringed. Charlie must have followed me back. I couldn't deal with this, I couldn't deal with him. I didn't see his car but he probably took a cab so no one would recognize him slumming it this side of New York. I wanted to run, and then changed my mind. I had a few things to say and then I would never have to speak to him again.

Gina noticed him too and menacingly reached into her pocket for what I am assuming was mace, or a knife. I don't know but she was a female shop owner in SoHo, so I'm sure she was prepared for anything.

"Hey, hey, its ok, I mean no harm! I just want to talk to Emmie." The man put his arms up as he stood up and walked towards us. Although his voice was very familiar, it wasn't Charlie. It was Jackson.

Being the protective motherly figure she was, Gina got in front of me and said, "Well, she has had enough men *talking* to her tonight, so you can just go back to where you came from."

"It's ok Gina, this is my friend Jackson. You remember him from the first day I came into the shop?"

"Well, I got this…" she held up a tiny bottle of mace and a rape whistle, "in case you get any bright ideas." She walked past Jackson and never took her eyes off of him. It was almost enough to make me laugh, but I still wasn't quite in the mood.

"Ok, what was that all about??" Jackson said.

"Oh, you know, rough night." I added and rolled my eyes. "What are you doing here Jackson?"

"That's the second time today you have said that to me Em. I'm gonna start getting a complex about the places I frequent." Even though his face looked angry, his voice had its usual sarcastic humor so I could tell he wasn't actually mad.

"Do you normally frequent empty buildings in the middle of the night?" I said, my words slurring from all of the alcohol finally catching up to me.

"Being as I was greeted with a can of mace in my face, I should probably rethink this particular neighborhood."

He had changed his outfit since this afternoon. He stood in front of me in his ripped and faded blue jeans that I loved and a Beatles t-shirt. I don't think I could've described a hotter man at that moment. But that could've been those four beers I had.

"So, what did she mean when she said you have had enough men talking to you already?" he asked, sounding a little more inquisitive than usual.

"Did the emergency at the shop include lots of men needing to question you?"

"Oh, right, the emergency." I had completely forgotten after everything that happened tonight. "Yeah, it wasn't a bad emergency, well not really. Gina wanted to tell me that she sold all of my jewelry." Just saying that out loud brought back all of the anger I felt at Charlie again.

"Wow Emmie, that's great!" He flashed me a genuine smile and I knew he really meant it. "You see, I told you not to be worried and everything would work out. I guess that explains the celebratory outfit. Not that I am going to complain for one second about seeing you in that, what is that, a dress? Bathing suit? Some sort of net for catching fish, perhaps?" His grin stretched all the way across his face as he looked me over. "So, you went out with the ladies to celebrate? Why don't you look ecstatic right now?"

"Because..." What should I say? Should I tell him about Charlie? What would he think? As tired and angry and wrung out as I felt, I didn't have it in me to lie. Plus, I was feeling just a tad drunk and that's usually when the truth tends to seep out.

"Because Charlie asked me to get back together with him earlier today and I actually thought about it. I mean, I was stupid enough to actually think about it." I stared down at his feet as I rambled on. The world was starting to spin and for some reason his black and white converses were the only thing on the earth that were standing still.

"And then I found out that he cheated on me with random women, well I actually don't know who the women were. It could've been anyone, who knows? I guess paint my face red because I'm an idiot who actually thought that being in a committed relationship meant something. But I am such a fool to have thought that for one second I wasn't 100% right when I left him. I knew it was the right thing to do, and I have always trusted my gut, but instead I let my insecurities cloud my head, and wow, my head is really clouded right now."

He hadn't said anything, but he was staring at me with this look on his face that I couldn't decipher. I took a shaky step back and I could feel my body leaning, but I was on a roll and there were things I just needed to say out loud. Not particularly to Jackson, but to the universe. And what better time than when the world seemed to be on a slight tilt.

"It's not that I ever even loved Charlie. I just think I loved the idea of him. The idea that someone with everything could still want *me*, who was nothing. A nobody. And he did. He wanted me and I accepted it all. Because who wants to live in the real world when you can have the fantasy, right? And who wants to live in a one room apartment above a consignment shop in SoHo, right?"

I raised my arm gesturing to the building behind me.

"Who wants this? I'll tell you who. Me, that's who! Me. And maybe I'm an idiot for wanting this when I could've had it all. But I guess I didn't really have anything, did I? Just one big empty apartment on Fifth Avenue to house my empty soul."

Tears started to fall down my cheeks because I couldn't contain them anymore. Before I could break down like I wanted to, Jackson grabbed me around the back and pulled me into his arms. Before I knew it, we were inside the shop, heading towards the steps to my room.

"Let's not have you standing on the street baring your soul to every hooligan walking past." He said as we walked past Gina who was fiddling with something behind the counter and looked up when she heard me crying. "There are people with mace around here you know."

I couldn't help but let out a loud laugh in the midst of my cries. "Ha! He was talking about you Gina."

"Aw, there's my clever girl. Come on, let's get you to bed before any more of that sharp wit comes spilling out all over the floor." He said as he led me up the stairs.

"Second door on the right," Gina said, sounding less than amused.

"Thanks." Jackson said, clicking his thumb and pointer finger at her like a gun. "And I cross my heart, I won't *talk* to her anymore tonight."

"Funny. So funny." I said, letting him guide me up the stairs to my room. "Why are you so funny all the time?"

"Coping mechanism. I use it to mask my irresistible male sexuality. I'm telling you, if I let you see what's really behind all of this humor, you would be sweating like a whore in church."

I laughed out loud again, and he looked at me seriously.

"Oh it's no joke Em. Walking down the street I'm like a fire. Girls just turn into puddles all around me. I'm a danger to society. Someone had to stop the insanity."

I could hear the smallest of giggles from the bottom of the stairs and it made me smile. Not many people surprised Gina, even fewer made her laugh like a little girl. I suppose he was right, he was a danger to women all over.

We reached my room in what seemed like a hundred and fifty five long steps. Since the door downstairs was kept locked, I never even bothered to shut the door to my room. He walked me in, as I was having trouble keeping my feet on the ground.

"This is it. My humble abode."

"Quite lovely indeed. Although," he gestured towards my tiny single bed, "I would've opted for a smaller bed. You know how I despise having enough room to lay any other way than curled up in the fetal position."

"I wouldn't know, you always slept on the couch." I whipped my arms out and fell on to the small bed right onto my back.

"Are you ok Em?" He asked with a small chuckle.

It was the second time I had been asked that question tonight but now I wasn't sure how to answer. I had been so brutally and openly honest already, and right now, I just wanted to swallow everything and make it all go away. I didn't want to burden Jackson anymore with my problems. He had saved me more times than I could ever think to repay him.

"Yes, I'm fine Jackson. You're here, so I'm fine." As soon as I said the words, I reached out and pulled him into my arms. I wasn't really sure what I was doing, but I knew I wanted him to hold me. Instinctively, I pulled my head back to look into his eyes and in that moment I wanted to kiss him more than anything in the world.

Sober me would've stopped to think of all of the reasons I shouldn't, but drunk me decided to go for it. I tilted my head, the clear international symbol for kiss me, leaned in, closed my eyes and apparently drifted off into a drunken slumber.

When I woke up, my head was still spinning, but the room was bright and empty. Not empty like it always was, empty because Jackson had gone. I don't know why I had thought he would stay. I passed out on him after exploding all of my emotional baggage with Charlie on to him and the streets of SoHo. Had I really expected him to be here when I woke up?

I slowly crawled out of bed and started peeling myself out of the thong-sicle I was wearing. I'm surprised my body hadn't just ingested it while I was sleeping for warmth. I flung it over my bed, pulled on a pair of black yoga pants and a t-shirt, and went downstairs to see if Gina had any of my favorite frosted doughnuts left over from yesterday.

"Hey," I said, as I saw her and Shirley slumped together waiting for the coffee maker to slowly drip black liquid into their cups.

"Uh," Shirley grunted and nodded at me.

"Do you have any..."

"Here," Shirley said, handing me a box. "I got some fresh ones on my way ovah."

It was amazing how in such a short amount of time, these ladies already knew me. All that time with Charlie and he had no idea who I was. I knew for a fact I would never second guess my decision again.

I grabbed one with white icing and pink sprinkles and shoved it into my mouth. Nothing can cure a hangover like a blob of fried dough smothered in sugar. Nothing.

"So, had I known you would be having two gorgeous men throwing themselves at you, I would've cancelled my subscription to the soap opera channel and just started watching your life." Gina said, giving me a look that asked for more information.

"What's this about two men? Did I miss something?" Shirley asked.

"You always miss stuff Shirl," Gina said, "but this last one was a gentleman. Not like that jackass at the club last night."

"I'm lost. You had *another* man here last night? Geez Louise, I need to start being your wing woman. You just cast off the ones you don't want and I will reel em in." Shirley threw her arm out like a fishing pole and started cranking in an oversized imaginary fish.

They both laughed.

"I don't know if I'd go jumping on my bandwagon just yet. I did sleep alone last night." I said as I popped the last bite of doughnut into my mouth.

"What happened to funny boy?" Gina asked. "That one, I could see maybe spending a little time with, if ya' know what I mean." She elbowed Shirley in the arm.

I thought about Jackson. I totally spilled my guts to him about wanting to get back together with Charlie, after he told me he had feelings for me. Then I tried to kiss him, unless by some miracle that was just a drunken hallucination. I was an idiot and he ran away. I mean, I didn't blame him, but I had always thought he was my go-to guy. He was always there to save me and make me laugh and feed me random comfort foods. Had I just messed up big time?

"I am not really sure. I kind of blurted a bunch of stuff out and then passed out on him. I'm guessing he is changing his locks and forgetting my phone number as we speak."

I casually left out the part about trying to suck face with him in hopes that it really was just a bad dream. I knew that I had made the right choice with Charlie, but I still wasn't sure about Jackson. Not that I even had a choice at this point. I doubt he would ever speak to me again.

"Nah, that boy looked at you like you were the last piece of cheesecake on the Earth. I don't think you could've spooked him with a little bit of tipsy talk." Gina smiled and Shirley looked at her with raised eyebrows.

"*Tipsy talk?* That's a good one Gina! I'm gonna have to use that from now on. 'Excuse me sir, do ya' mind if you and I have ourselves some *tipsy talk?*'" She laughed so hard at herself she snorted, which had both of them laughing again.

Just watching them together made me realize it had been an excruciatingly long time since I had even spoken to my best friend back home. And since my girls night out hadn't done its job of clearing my thoughts, I knew there was only one person who would be able to help me out of this emotional impasse.

"Ladies, if you will excuse me, I have a long awaited phone call I have to make." I started up the stairs to my room but stopped to make a U-turn to grab a doughnut for the road.

As I climbed the stairs I heard Shirley call after me, "If there are any fish on the line that you are tossing back in the water, give em my number!"

Chapter 13.....

"Well, look who finally decided to touch down off cloud nine to give us common folk a call."

"Amy…" Just hearing her voice made me feel warm again. "I just, I have missed you."

I almost started to cry, but I held it in as much as I could. I really did miss her. I missed a lot, but my best friend was definitely at the top of that list.

"Ok, it must be bad. What's wrong?" Amy knew me better than anyone I had ever known, so hiding things from her were always difficult.

Why had I waited so long to call her? Oh yeah, because I didn't want her to know how much of a mess I had made of my perfect fairy tale life.

"It's a long and overwhelming story, which I'm sure you don't have time for."

"Mark and the kids are at his mom's house, so I've got all the time in the world for you. Spill it."

After filling her in on the mess that was my life the past few weeks, she said nothing. Moments went by as I waited for her to scream at me, cry with me, or just tell me something and just as I was about to blurt out "say something!", she cleared her throat and said, "Well, New York must have some really good coffee." Then she laughed.

"Amy!" I yelled, but couldn't help but laugh with her. It was just so good to talk to her.

"Oh Em, I know it's been a while since you have been home, but I didn't realize that big city could wipe away all of your common sense."

"What is that supposed to mean?" Did she think I was lying to myself about Charlie? "I never would've thought he was going to cheat on me. I mean, I had my doubts as to why *he* wanted to be with *me*, but…"

"That's not what I'm talking about. That jerk doesn't deserve another second of your time, and if I was able to come up there, I would tell that to him myself, right after I climbed up on a stool and punched him in the face."

That made both of us laugh. She was about a foot shorter than I was, and I could barely reach to put my arms around Charlie. "No Em, I'm talking about this artist guy. What did you say his name was, Jackson, right?"

"Oh yeah. Uh-huh. What about him?"

"*Esmerelda Rose Duncan!*" she yelled into the phone.

I hated when anyone called me by my full name, and it had been a long time since I had heard it, but Amy was allowed to do things normal people couldn't. She had been my best friend since we were little, and she knew things, things that no one else knew. Things that needed to go with her to the grave. So, she was allowed to call me whatever she wanted.

"When did you lose all of those intelligent brain cells my mother always told me she wished would rub off onto me? How is it that you can't even see that this man is insanely in love with you?"

"Oh no, no, no, no. I must have given you the wrong impression about Jackson, I mean he said he was attracted to me, but we hardly know each other, and..."

"Seriously. I know how you have always thought less of yourself my dear, but most of us on the planet can see that you are a total hottie. Not to mention you are amazing and smart and all around fabulous. But yes, a total hottie as well."

Though she couldn't see me through the phone, I think she knew I was already about to argue with her so she quickly added, "Don't you dare try to tell me otherwise Emmie, because although I am your very best friend in the whole world and have been there through some very bad hair days and unfortunate outfit choices, I can still see how wonderful you are. And that is why that lying, cheating dirt bag Charlie fell in love with you, even if he was a loser. And that is why this Jackson guy, who I would really like to meet because he sounds dreamy, is head over heels for you."

I didn't even know what to say. I had never really thought of myself as someone worthy of such a perfect love, which is why I constantly second guessed my "fairy tale" relationship with Charlie. I always thought he was too good for me and I suppose I wasn't all that surprised that he had cheated on me. As for Jackson, I never really thought of him as anything more than a friend, but it was starting to come clear to me that I was lying to myself. He was way more than a friend. At least I wanted him to be. I know he said he was attracted to me, but could that have changed?

"Even if Jackson actually liked me, I'm pretty sure I blew it last night, pouring my heart out about Charlie and then throwing myself at him, only to have him walk out on me." Remembering the events of last night still stung in my already hung-over head.

"I know you have been shacked up with that Richie Rich low life for so long that you might not have remembered what a gentleman is, but that is what you witnessed last night. Any decent man is not going to take advantage of a drunken woman who is obviously acting out of her mind, Emmie. Oh and by the way, I am absolutely devastated that I didn't get to see you drunk. This is something we need to rectify immediately. I think of all people I deserve to be there for these milestones in your life!"

We laughed together again. This phone call was exactly what I needed. I felt so bad that I hadn't called her sooner.

"Amy, I'm sorry it's been so long since I called. I just didn't want to have to tell you how screwed up my life had become. I know how you always said you envied the fabulous life Charlie and I had together. I didn't want you to know that everything wasn't as story book as it seemed."

"Emmie, first of all, you *should* apologize for not calling. I mean, that was just rude. Secondly, the reason you just gave for *not* calling is lame, and hurts my feelings. I know it may not be as glorious as Fifth Avenue, but I really do love my life. Crazy kids, dirty laundry, goofy small town husband and all."

Wow I felt like a jerk. "I didn't mean it like that, I..."

"No, no, no, you said it. Yes, I have mentioned before how I was a little jealous of your new life in the big city, but that doesn't mean that I would give up my life for anything. I mean, I might temporarily trade my swollen ankles and the constant kicking of my ribs from the inside, but I would miss even that."

"Amy, I am so sorry. Of course you love your life. I love your life. I wish I had your life. The past few weeks have just been so emotionally exhausting, I don't even know where my head is."

"It's not your head you should be worried about right now. Your heart needs to be what is leading you. And my head is telling me that your heart should be making another phone call right after this one."

"I don't even know what to say to him. Do I apologize? Do I tell him, what? What do I say? I mean, I don't even know how I feel." Was that true?

"I swear, this conversation has been like pulling teeth Emmie." I could almost hear her eyes rolling through the phone. "Am I the only one here who can see love when it is smacking two people in the face?"

"Love?"

"Yes, love. Lovey dovey smoochie woochie love Em. You are in love with this man, and I must say, from the very little I have already heard about him, I think it is a very good thing. You have always needed someone to challenge you, which is why *we* are such amazing friends. But as much as it pains me to say, this isn't about me. This is about you and how you always run away from the things in your life that scare you."

"That is not true! I was terrified of Charlie and I let myself fall in love with him. We all know how well that worked out." My heart just kept twisting and turning the more I thought about it.

"Charlie was not a challenge. You weren't afraid of him because he was what you had always dreamed of, minus the whole cheating bastard aspect. It's easy to fall in love with a fantasy. Not so easy to love someone who is tough. Jackson is difficult. He challenges you in ways that scare you, but that is exactly what you need."

"You think I need to be challenged? What about living the easy life? Aren't you the one telling me that I need to stop being so hard on myself? Now I need a man who is tough on me?"

"Yes, be a little easier on yourself, but get yourself a man who will challenge you. You get bored way too easily Emmie. I know you want to live in this beautiful fantasy world where a man sweeps you off your feet and you ride off into the sunset together, but come on. Those men do not exist, and if they did, you would get bored in about thirty seconds."

"I don't think.."

"Exactly, that's why you called me, isn't it?" I could hear her smiling. I'm glad she was getting some enjoyment out of this. I was more confused than ever. Although there was one thing I was becoming increasingly sure of, I had a lot of thinking to do about Jackson.

"Ok, so let's say I call Jackson and he hangs up on me because of the fool I made of myself coming on to him last night. Then what?"

"This guy let you cry on his shoulder after you left your boyfriend on one knee with a ring in his hand. He gives you a place to sleep, and sleeps on the couch no less, buys you new clothes to wear, helps you get back on your feet, writes songs about you…"

"Wait, I didn't say the song was about me, I just said I kind of wanted it to be."

"Ok, he totally wrote that song about you, and quit interrupting me."

"My lips are sealed."

"So, he does all of these things, and then you go all bat crazy on him and tell him to grow up, and that you are moving out. He still professes his feelings for you, then rescues you after a crappy night and does the gentlemanly thing and lets you sleep it off instead of taking advantage of you. And you are worried that he might hang up on you because you possibly offended him by throwing yourself at him? Really Em? Do I need to spell it out for you yet again? This dude is in love with you. I should know. If I didn't love you, I wouldn't put up with you."

"Well, thanks Amy."

"I told ya, I love you. I don't need to sugar coat it. And if I was the kind of friend who did, you would get bored of me too. Thus, bringing us back to my point, he is clearly the one."

"The one? You think he is the one? You haven't even met him? I didn't even know until half way through this conversation that I even really liked him and now you're saying he's the one?" I was sort of blown away at how sure she could be.

"Listen, when you've been married as long as I have, you learn a few things. You learn that as a woman, you get to be right way less often than you did when you were just dating; you are ultimately promoted to laundry duties even if you have a full time job, and you learn that best friends know more than you do about your life. So basically what I am saying is, suck it, listen to me, call that man and tell him to take you to dinner."

How was I supposed to argue with that? I knew I really needed to think about everything she had said, but I also knew that Amy was usually right, and that I have always listened to her advice.

As if she could actually read my mind, she said, "Don't bother getting those gears in your head turning, you know you always listen to me."

"Why is it that I always listen to you?"

"Because even though you are smarter than me, I am wiser."

"That doesn't make any sense."

"That's because you're not as wise as I am."

And then we were laughing again.

"You really need to call me more. I have really missed you Em."

"I really missed you too. I'm sorry. I promise I won't let anything else get in the way of our relationship. And besides, I expect to get a call from you when that baby is here. Well, maybe not from you personally, if you're in labor and all. I suppose you could have Mark call me."

"I can guarantee you I will have someone call you. However, I plan on being in an epidural coma in which the baby miraculously slides out of my body without disturbing me whatsoever. Also, since my mother in law is planning on keeping the kids while I give birth, I was thinking I might just go in early and get a mom-cation from my demon spawn before I add another one to the mix."

"Mom-cation? Amy, you make having children sound like such a blessing. Give my two favorite tiny humans a big smooch from me, ok?"

"Just as soon as I finish this glass of wine and enjoy the quiet of them being at Nana's. Anyway, we were not done here lady. What are you going to do when you hang up this phone?"

I knew what she wanted me to say. I knew what I wanted to do. I just didn't know if I had the guts to do it, or deal with the consequences of it when I did.

"I am going to call Jackson and…"

"No, no, no. First, you are going to take a deep breath, and then a shower. Because although I can't smell you, I'm pretty sure you haven't showered since before your night of drinking and if this phone call goes as I hope it does, you will want to look and smell your best. And then, only then, will you pick up that phone and tell this hot piece of man meat, wait, he is a hot piece of man meat, right?"

I actually hadn't given it too much thought until lately. Picturing him in my head in jeans and a t-shirt with his messy hair and that sweet musky smell that always lingered on his clothes; I couldn't help but get a big smile on my face.

"Yes, I suppose he is a hot piece of man meat Amy."

"Yeah, that's what I thought." I could hear her smiling. "So, as I was saying, you are going to call that hottie and tell him that you were a drunken idiot last night but it made you realize your true feelings for him. And those feelings would like to be sextified."

"Sextified?"

"Being satisfied by some hot steamy sex. Has it really been that long Em?"

"Unfortunately, yes it has. But that's not what I want from Jackson. Well, I don't really even know what I want from him. Since you seem to be the expert, why don't you tell me? What exactly do I want from him, besides some sextification?"

"Now you're getting it," she started laughing. "You want him to rock your world, then put a rock on your finger. It's as simple as that."

As simple as that, huh? It sounded like the most complicated conversation I would ever have, besides breaking up with ass face Charlie. Man, it felt really good calling him that.

"And you really think this is what he wants too?"

"Well, being that I have no idea who he is and have never met him, I'm not one hundred percent, but if history has proven anything to us, I am always right. Listen Em, we have been over this already. Quit second guessing yourself, and me, and call that man!"

"Ok."

"Ok. And then call me back and tell me everything. We got rid of cable so I need some juicy entertainment. Now go. Love you."

"Love you too. Thank you."

As I hung up the phone, I couldn't help but feel happy, but also insanely petrified. I knew she was right, I had to call Jackson. But that meant owning up to my true feelings and apologizing for being such a crybaby loser last night. Acknowledging I had let my emotions get the better of me was never an easy thing to admit, but if nothing else, Jackson was owed an apology.

There was also another thing Amy was right about. I needed a long, hot shower. Maybe the hot water would help clear my head. Or maybe I would drown and I could enjoy the quiet, pleasurable bliss of death. Both sounded like fairly balanced options at this point.

Chapter 14...

After almost a half hour soaking under the steady stream of hot water in the shower, my skin was wrinkled but my head was a little clearer. As much as I didn't want to admit it to myself, I was fairly certain that Amy was right. I was in love with Jackson, and I suppose I had been for a while.

I was even more nervous about calling him than before. It was one thing to tell him I was sorry for acting like an idiot, yet another to tell him the reason was because I was madly in love with him. I had never been afraid of how he would react to anything I did or said before because I always thought no matter what he would still be my friend. Now I was asking him not to be my friend anymore. Would he laugh in my face?

I wiped the steam away from the mirror and looked at myself. Trying to visualize myself as a hottie, as Amy put it, was never going to happen. Not that I thought I was ugly, just plain. Plain and ordinary. And I certainly never thought ordinary, plain Jane, Esmerelda Rose Duncan would stand a chance in hell with extraordinary, artsy, funny, gorgeous, wonderful Jackson, don't know his middle name, Thomas.

He could really have his pick of the most amazing girls out there. He had the whole uptown thing going for him with his infinite real estate knowledge and witty repartee, not to mention he looked fantastic in a suit and tie. Then there was his artistic, write you a song, paint you a picture, bake you a cake side that would have every woman starry-eyed and swooning. And Amy was right; I had never once been bored with him. He was captivating. And when he wasn't, he was downright vexing, but I loved every second of it. How did it take me this long to see?

I dried off from the long shower, put on a nice pair of jeans, my fanciest t-shirt, and flipped my hair up in a loose bun. It was one of those I look like I just rolled out of bed but you know I secretly tried to look good looks. I didn't want to look like I was trying too hard, but I had to hide the train wreck that was bubbling up to the surface of my psyche. If Jackson came over, I had to give him some sort of reason to want to choose me.

After grooming myself more extensively than a prize pony, I grabbed my phone and shakily dialed Jackson's number. I had already gone over what I was going to say to him about a hundred times in the shower and while I was getting ready, but my nerves were still in full force as the phone started ringing.

And it rang, and it rang, and it rang, until his voicemail picked up. Hearing that sweet voice gave me goose bumps and I almost forgot that at the end of his message I was going to have to say something. When he stopped talking and the quintessential beep came on my end, I stuttered a little and just spit out, "Jackson, it's Emmie, um, just please give me a call when you get a chance. Thank you."

Yeah, that'll win him over.

Waiting for a man to call never gets easier. I remember sitting by the phone in my bedroom when I was fifteen because Miles Kenderson, the most amazingly gorgeous junior and star soccer player, asked Amy for my phone number in homeroom. I waited for almost a week, and each day was agonizing. I had imaginary conversations with him in my head that always ended with us professing our undying love to one another. When he finally got around to calling, the only thing he asked me was if I had the notes from algebra. Apparently I took the best notes.

Jackson didn't call me that day. I thought about calling him again but I knew I wouldn't have anything better to say to his voicemail if he didn't answer, and I didn't want to seem too desperate, even though I suppose I was. The bad thing about cell phones is that most people have them at all times, so I was pretty sure Jackson had gotten my message. The fact that he didn't call me right away wasn't the best sign.

I had spent most of my day just hanging around my room above the shop. I was nursing a slight hangover and trying to get the events of the past few days straightened out in my head. I tried not to think about Jackson, but the only other thing that crept into my mind was Charlie and that was not a subject I wanted to delve into any deeper. He had cheated on me. My perfect prince Charming had cheated on me. If that could happen, who's to say that I would ever find true love?

My theories on love had always been to find the fairy tale. I wanted someone to sweep me off of my feet and ride off into the sunset together. Now everything I had ever believed in was shattered. And here I was chasing after a man who was completely imperfect, who got on my nerves and challenged me at every turn. How was I supposed to believe that we could turn that into a fairy tale ending?

The afternoon was a haze of attempting to read, dozing off, and checking my phone for any resemblance of a response from Jackson. It was a good thing I had absolutely no social life to disturb my big day.

Finally at around 6pm, there was a knock on my door. My heart leapt up in my chest as I ran to open it, but standing on the other side was not who I expected.

"Charlie, what the hell are you…"

"Emmie, please don't slam the door in my face. I really need to talk to you."

"What gives you the right to come here to my home?"

"Home?" He scoffed. "This isn't your home Em."

I reached to shut the door. "I can't deal with this right now."

"Emmie, wait, please, I want to apologize." He stood in the doorway so I couldn't close it. "I should have listened to you. Last night I was a complete idiot."

"Now that is something I will not disagree with you on, however I would add jerk, creep, scumbag, bastard..." I couldn't think of anymore off the top of my head, but I'm sure if given the time I could've called him every name in the book, and he would've deserved it.

"I guess I deserve that." He said, as if reading my mind.

"Damn right you do!" I was getting worked up just having him standing in front of me. I didn't fully realize how much I was hurt by him, and how that even though just yesterday I thought I might have wanted him back in my life, at this moment, I hated him.

"You know what Charlie? I was seriously thinking that I had messed everything up. That it was some big mistake on my part walking out on you the night you proposed. That I was throwing away this magnificent thing. I suppose I should thank you for showing me that as usual, my instincts were right. I thought you were special, I thought I was special to you." I bit back the tears I felt welling in my eyes. I would not let him see me cry. As Amy said, he didn't deserve my tears ever again.

"That's just it, you are special to me. I was the one who made a mistake. I made a few mistakes. I didn't have faith in you before, but now I do. I took you for granted, but I promise I won't ever do that again. Just give me a chance Emmie."

Before I could tell him off yet again, he grabbed my face in both hands and tried to kiss me. I was so shocked at what he was doing that I didn't even hear the footsteps coming up the stairs. I stared in disbelief at Charlie who was 2 inches away from my face. He pressed his lips to mine and felt my heart drop as I heard the voice I had wanted to hear all day.

"Oh, I'm sorry to interrupt."

"Oh my God, Jackson, no this is not..." I pushed Charlie away from me, but he barely moved.

He looked at Jackson with a small smile on his face that made me hate him so much more than I had before. "Yeah, sorry hoss, we were in the middle of something here."

"No we weren't. Charlie, you were leaving and I never want to see you again."

Jackson was already turned around and started walking down the stairs. I couldn't let this happen. I couldn't let Charlie wreck everything for me. He had already broken my heart, and now it looked as though he had broken Jackson's as well.

"Please Jack, wait."

"No, it's okay Emmie. It's obvious you need to sort some stuff out. I made a mistake coming here, I just..." he trailed off and slowly moved down the stairs.

I pushed Charlie back hard and ran over to Jackson. I felt sick to my stomach. How was I going to fix this? I had to fix this.

Charlie followed me. "Emmie, let this loser go. We have a lot we need to talk about."

At that, Jackson stopped and turned around. "Excuse me? Did I just hear you call *me* a loser?"

"I didn't stutter, did I?" Charlie spit out at him. "I think you've had enough fun shacking up with my girlfriend. Now I think it's time for you to run along and let us sort this out on our own, huh pal." He pushed Jackson's shoulder back.

"Are you kidding me right now?" Jackson looked about as stunned as I was. I had never seen Charlie acting like this. "I am pretty sure that you were the jerk she ran out on and came running to me."

Wow, I was standing smack dab in the middle of a real life pissing contest. "Both of you stop it. Charlie, you need to leave, now."

"Emmie, I'm not leaving you here with this low life. We have a lot we need to sort out." He reached to hold my hand but I pulled it back.

"We are done here. You need to leave." I backed myself against the wall to clear a path for him to go down the stairs. "I mean it, Charlie, go!"

"Fine. But we both know that you will come running back to me Emmie. I am what is good for you. So, when you are done slumming with this clown, you know where to find me." With that he pushed past Jackson and left.

"Jack, I'm so sorry, I..."

"Emmie, I should probably go too."

"No, don't go. Please, I really need to talk to you about last night, and God, I didn't know he was coming here today, or that he would try to..."

"You don't need to explain. You have a lot on your plate and you need to sort it all out. Which is why I should go." He started down the stairs again.

I grabbed his arm and felt a jolt of electricity in my hand as his skin touched mine. "I don't need to think about anything. Charlie is out of my life. I called you to tell you that. I wanted to apologize for unloading on you last night too. I wasn't thinking straight but now I am."

"That's the thing, I don't think you are Em. I think you need to think about what you want, about what you need in your life right now."

"What I need is..." At that moment, I didn't have the courage to say what I wanted to say. I thought I did, but what if he didn't feel the same way? What if he just wanted to be friends? I profess my love and he just wants to be friends. I don't think my heart could take that. Not today. "What I need is to talk to you."

"Okay then, talk." He crossed his arms over his chest.

That wasn't the response I had anticipated, but it was what I wanted. I didn't want him to leave.

"Well, do you think we could move from the stairs?"

I reached my hand out to him and I felt that same surge through my body when he softly placed his hand in mine. I led him up to my room and closed the door behind us. We both stood there awkwardly. I got him here, now what was I going to say to him?

He wasn't looking at me directly, and that was strange because he normally stared at me like he was seeing right into my soul. I couldn't tell if it was because he was nervous like me, or because he was upset with me. He had walked in on what looked like me kissing my ex.

I walked past him and sat on the bed, urging him to do the same.

He slowly sat down next to me. Still not looking at me, he took in a long deep breath. "Ok, so, you wanted to talk?"

"Yes, I did. I do." The question was could I say what I needed to say without screwing it all up? And what would he say?

"I didn't ask him to come here, you know that right? And I certainly didn't ask him to kiss me."

"Well, he wouldn't be my first choice to lock lips with, but you didn't seem to mind, until I showed up." His attitude had suddenly turned angry with that statement. "Listen, I understand you are confused, but I told you that I liked you, and I'm not just going to sit around watching you get back together with that tool. I don't even know what you saw in him in the first place. "

This was not the direction I wanted this conversation to go. I had to find a way to turn it around. "I'm not getting back together with him, ever. I don't even want to see him ever again. You're right, he is a tool."

"Well, of course I'm right. I'm always right." He smiled but his voice still had an edge to it.

"You do seem to have an annoying habit of always being right. But my giving you an ego boost was not what I wanted to talk to you about. I tried calling you because I wanted to talk about last night."

I could feel tension still lurking in the air, but I felt like if I didn't speak my mind now, he could walk away forever.

"So, about last night, you were right in leaving. At first, I was upset that you just left like that, but I…"

"Wait, you were upset with me for leaving? Emmie, you passed out." He let out a tiny laugh which helped calm my nerves a little.

"I know. I'm so sorry about that. I know how it must've seemed. First I throw myself at you and then I pass out."

"You threw yourself at me?" He looked in my eyes and smiled his adorable crooked Jackson smile. I wanted to squash my face into his.

"Well, I don't know. I thought I did. Didn't I?"

"Not to my recollection. And I'm usually pretty perceptive on those things." He looked down at his hands. "I remember a lot of talk about your ex though."

"Yes, I do remember that, and again, I'm sorry. But most of that was because he had just told me that our entire relationship was a lie. Oh and that he had cheated on me God knows how many times." No matter how many times I said it out loud, that still dug a hole in my chest.

"Listen Emmie, I knew you had some baggage when you came through my door that night in that phenomenal black dress. I didn't really know to what extent until right now, but that's why I think you need some time, and space, to figure stuff out. Coming here today was a mistake."

He got up to leave and I couldn't let that happen.

I hadn't rehearsed these next words, they came to me as I was talking but I knew as soon as I said them that they were the truth.

"It wasn't a mistake. Charlie was the mistake. I know I didn't tell you everything about mine and Charlie's relationship, but with him it felt like I had moved away from one parent and moved in with another. He told me what to do, how to dress, where to go. I wasn't myself anymore. Charlie wanted me to be this person who cared about things. I don't care about things, I care about people. I told myself it was ok because he loved me and I didn't want to be alone. But what is worse than being alone is being with someone who just doesn't get you, ya know? I mean, of course you don't know because you get me, you've always just gotten me. I think it took me meeting you to remember that I was a person that could exist separately from a relationship."

"Well, then you should do that. You should take some time to be alone so you can figure out what it is you want."

"No Jack, that's not what I'm saying."

"Yes, but it is what I'm saying. Listen, I like you Emmie, but when I saw you standing there with him, it just made me realize that I was being selfish coming here. I can't just expect you to jump from one ship to another when you haven't even worked out your feelings. Don't get me wrong, when I saw him getting ready to kiss you, I wanted to punch that ass hat in the face." He raised his eyebrows and cracked his knuckles.

"Ass hat?" I couldn't help but laugh.

"Yes, he is a total ass hat. But this isn't about the ass hat, and it isn't about me. Emmie, I think for anything to work out in your life, you need to step back, take a breath and find yourself. Find that person that is lurking just under the surface of this girl who sacrifices her own hopes and dreams trying to make everyone else happy. The girl who says I'm sorry a thousand times a day because God forbid she should ever offend anyone, even at the expense of herself. Emmie, you are on the verge of becoming the person you were meant to be, and I know that person is going to be astounding and magical and breathtaking. And if I can be a part of that in any way, then I will consider myself one lucky guy. But you can't find your amazing self when you are too busy trying to be what you think someone else wants."

I couldn't believe the words he was saying. They were beautiful and amazing, and yet they were ripping my heart out at the same time. I had just realized my feelings and was terrified to tell him, but I didn't have to worry about that now because he was walking away anyway.

"Jack, I..." I grabbed his hand because I couldn't find the words to keep him here. If I just held on, he couldn't walk away.

He pulled me into his arms for a hug. I was immediately bombarded with that intoxicating smell that always emanated from him. How could a person smell so good you physically wanted to eat them? I wrapped myself up in him, not ever wanting to let go. Not wanting to surrender to what I knew was about to happen.

"I swear to you Emmie, you are just beginning to see what this life has in store for you." He stroked my hair like he did that first night in his apartment, when I had told him about breaking up with Charlie and we spent the night eating chocolate cake on the roof. That night I thought my life was over, that I had ruined everything that would ever make me happy. And it was this man who was holding me in his arms who helped me realize that there would be life after Fifth Avenue.

How could I just let him go?

"You tell me I'm supposed to find myself, then why do I feel like I'm losing a piece of me?" I whispered it into his chest, not really saying it loud enough for him to hear me, but he still did.

"Oh kid, you aren't going to lose me." He pulled me back and tipped my chin up to look in his face. "You should know you can't get rid of me that easily."

I stared into his eyes for longer than I could even remember. I would've thought it would be awkward, but it wasn't. I could feel my chest constricting. He was right, of course he was right. I had to work on my own stuff before I could even think about getting into another relationship. It didn't make any of it easy, and I knew that no matter what, I would fight to have Jackson in my life. But I didn't want this to happen. I didn't want him to leave me, even if it was for the best right now.

"I should probably get going. I have a grown-up meeting tomorrow and I have to find the one tie I own and make sure I can still tie it."

He stood up and on impulse I stood up with him. It wasn't a polite gesture, I just didn't want his space to move away from my space.

He looked down at me again and smiled. "If you ever find yourself in a small black dress in the middle of the night, you obviously know where to find me."

He slowly moved toward the door. I was about to be alone all over again. I wouldn't let this be the end of me and Jackson, but my heart was still breaking. I had to say something, anything. Nothing was coming to mind except to tell him to stay and I knew I couldn't ask that. I had to let him go. If you love something set it free right? Whoever the dummy was who thought of that I could punch in the face.

"A dream you dream alone is only a dream. A dream you dream together is reality." I figured only John Lennon could say what I needed to say at this moment. While saying those words, I could feel the tears falling down my cheeks.

And just when I thought this moment would go down in history as the worst of my life so far, he leaned his head down, wiped the tears from my cheeks and whispered in my ear my absolute favorite Lennon quote of all time. "It'll all be okay in the end. If it's not okay, it's not the end."

Then he pressed his lips onto mine.